BILLY SURE

•KID ENTREPRENEUR•

AND THE CAT-DOG TRANSLATOR

INVENTED BY **LUKE SHARPE**

DRAWINGS BY **GRAHAM ROSS**

Simon Spotlight

New York London Toronto Sydney New Delhi

This book is a work of fiction. Any references to historical events, real people, or real places are used fictitiously. Other names, characters, places, and events are products of the author's imagination, and any resemblance to actual events or places or persons, living or dead, is entirely coincidental.

SIMON SPOTLIGHT

An imprint of Simon & Schuster Children's Publishing Division

1230 Avenue of the Americas, New York, New York 10020

First Simon Spotlight paperback edition September 2015

Copyright © 2015 by Simon & Schuster, Inc. Text by Michael Teitelbaum.
Illustrations by Graham Ross. All rights reserved, including the right of reproduction in whole or in part in any form.

SIMON SPOTLIGHT and colophon are registered trademarks of Simon & Schuster, Inc.

For information about special discounts for bulk purchases, please contact Simon & Schuster Special Sales at 1-866-506-1949 or business@simonandschuster.com.

Designed by Jay Colvin

The text of this book was set in Minya Nouvelle.

Manufactured in the United States of America 0715 OFF

10 9 8 7 6 5 4 3 2 1

ISBN 978-1-4814-4762-1 (hc)

ISBN 978-1-4814-4761-4 (pbk)

ISBN 978-1-4814-4763-8 (eBook)

Library of Congress Catalog Number 2014954731

Chapter One

a Boy and His Dog

MY NAME IS BILLY SURE. I'M AN INVENTOR. I'm also the CEO of my very own company: SURE THINGS, INC. You might have heard of our products. You might even have some of them.

The ALL BALL that changes into different sports balls with the touch of a button? That's us. The SIBLING SILENCER that, well, silences siblings? Yep, us too. DISAPPEARING REAPPEARING MAKEUP and STINK SPEC-TACULAR? Well, you get the picture. Sure Things, Inc. has had one success after another.

ALL BALL
small

ALL BALL
large

SIBLING SILENCER

The best *part* of being in business is my business *partner*. Get it? Manny Reyes is my best friend and Chief Financial Officer (CFO for short), which is a fancy way of saying that he takes care of money while I create inventions. Manny's a genius when it comes to marketing, numbers, planning, selling, advertising, computers. . . .

I could go on. But basically, I invent our products and Manny figures out how to make them into hits. It's a bit more complicated than that, but in a nutshell, that's our story.

It's a Tuesday evening. I'm home after a full day at school, followed by a full day at work. It's not easy juggling two lives.

My typical day is: Get up (I suppose you could have guessed that part, right?); shower; go to school; come home and pick up my dog, Philo; then go with Philo to the World Headquarters of Sure Things, Inc. (also known as Manny's garage). Then I come home, eat dinner, do my homework, maybe read a book or watch TV, and then go to sleep.

And you thought you were busy with soccer and school plays and—well, I guess you're busy too. I don't mean to complain—it's just that sometimes all this gets a bit overwhelming. That's when I have to remember how much I enjoy inventing stuff.

At this moment, I'm in the "finished school, finished work, finished dinner, finished homework" portion of my day. I'm hanging out in the living room playing with Philo.

"You want this, boy?" I ask, leaning forward in my seat, waving Philo's favorite chew toy at him. It's a thick rope made up of colored strands all woven together. Or at least they used to be woven together. Months of chewing and pulling have taken their toll.

Philo jumps up from his doggy bed on the

other side of the room, dashes over to where I'm sitting, and grabs one end of the toy in his teeth.

I yank my end back. Philo bares his teeth and growls, a low growl that's as much a moan or a whine as a true growl.

"Who's a FIERCE BEAST?" I ask, moving the toy—and Philo's head along with it—from side to side.

Philo tugs hard, pulling me from my chair. I tumble to the rug and start laughing. Letting go of my end of the toy, I rub Philo's belly. This always makes him go a little crazy.

I roll over, and then Philo jumps on top of me. We tumble across the room, me laughing, Philo growling and barking.

"What's going on down there?!" shouts a voice from upstairs. "Some of us have homework to do, y'know!"

That would be Emily, my sister. Last week, Emily only spoke in a British accent. Before that, she only wore black. Who knows what she'll be into next?

"Just playing with Philo," I call back up the stairs.

"Well, do it quietly!" she screams down.

I pick up Philo's chew toy and hold it over my head.

"Do you want this, boy?" I say in an excited whisper, waving the colorful, floppy rope back and forth.

Philo's head follows the moving rope, as if he were watching a Ping-Pong match.

"Ready?" I ask.

Philo backs up a few steps.

"Go get it!" I shout, tossing the rope over his head.

Philo turns and dashes after the rope. He snatches it up in his mouth, then trots contentedly back toward me, dropping it at my feet.

"Again?" I ask.

"RUUFFF!" he replies.

Sometimes I can almost understand what Philo is saying.

I pick up the rope and waggle it back and forth, then fling it past him.

This time Philo turns his head casually and watches the rope zoom by, then he turns back to look at me.

So much for understanding what Philo says.

"I thought you wanted to play, boy?" I say.

Philo stares at me like he's never seen me before.

"Go get it!" I say again.

Philo continues staring.

Oh well. I walk to the other side of the room, pick up the toy, and come back.

"One more time." I toss the rope back over Philo's head. It bounces a couple of times, then disappears into the dining room.

This time Philo turns and chases after it. He speeds from the living room into the dining room. And then doesn't come back.

"Get the toy, Philo!" I shout.

No Philo. No toy.

"Bring me the toy, Philo!" I yell again.

"Go get the stupid toy yourself!" Emily shouts from upstairs.

She totally does not get the point of this game.

But she may be right. I'm beginning to wonder where Philo went. As I step from the living room into the dining room, I find the chew toy sitting on the floor. Looking up, I see that Philo is all the way on the other side of the room.

"It's right here, boy," I say, pointing down at the toy.

Philo paces back and forth across the floor on the far side of the dining room. He stops, sniffs under some furniture, then turns and walks back to the other side of the room, where he repeats the sniffing, then the pacing, then the sniffing, and on and on.

As he paces and sniffs, Philo lets out a series of low moans and short yelps.

"URRRR . . . YIP-YIP!" he says.

"What is it, boy?" I ask.

"**URRRR . . . YIP-YIP!**" he repeats.

Now I really wish I could understand what Philo is saying. In fact, there have been many times when I've wished I could understand him. Things would be so much easier. I could just give him what he wants and he'd be happy. And then I wouldn't spend so much time wondering what he's trying to say.

And that's when it hits me. I know what Sure Things, Inc.'s next product should be! I will make a translator for dogs!

This isn't the first time this invention idea has come up. The first time I ever thought of it, I had just discovered the blueprints for the Sibling Silencer on my desk, but I didn't know where they had come from. Let me explain. . . .

You see, I always have trouble figuring out how to make my inventions work . . . at least when I'm awake. When I finally give up and go to sleep, the completed blueprints MAGICALLY appear on my desk the next morning.

You may be wondering who so kindly and

quietly draws the blueprints for me in the middle of the night. I wondered the same thing at first. It turns out that *I* do! In my sleep! Here's how we found out.

My first invention, the All Ball, was a hit, but I didn't know where the working blueprints came from. They had appeared on my desk one morning, and I didn't recognize the handwriting. So when I was struggling to come up with the working blueprints for Sure Things, Inc.'s next invention, the Sibling Silencer, Manny rigged an alarm system so that whoever was sneaking into my room to leave the blueprints would get caught. Except the only one who tripped the alarm was Philo. When he did, I discovered new blueprints on my desk, which meant that Philo saw who put them there.

What I didn't know was that Manny also set up a webcam and watched me work on the blueprints in my sleep. That's right. Some people talk in their sleep; some people walk in their sleep; but me, I invent things in my sleep!

But before I knew that, I remember wishing at that moment for a device that could translate what Philo was saying through his barks. And that's when the idea for the DOG TRANSLATOR first came into my head.

I have to tell Manny about this! The time has arrived for the Dog Translator!

I start to head up to my room to send Manny an e-mail, when I hear Philo scraping his paw against the floor. Turning back, I see him reach under a cabinet and drag out a doggy treat. A dust-covered, stale treat.

That thing must have been under there for weeks! Philo happily munches away.

Yuck! Dogs can be really gross sometimes.

See, if I had a Dog Translator, Philo could have just told me he wanted a treat. Of course, Philo doesn't need a translator for that. Like most dogs, he *always* wants a treat!

I dash up the stairs. I have to pass Emily's room in order to get to mine.

"What? You're done making noise downstairs, so you decided to come here and make

noise upstairs?" she asks in her usual warm, loving tone.

"The lightbulb just went off!" I say, pointing to my head, hardly able to contain my excitement.

Emily shrugs without looking up from her desk. "So ask Dad to replace it, genius."

"No, I mean I just came up with the idea for my next invention," I say, smiling.

"Uh-huh," she replies, tapping away on her phone, her thumbs blazing. "I'll alert the media."

"Actually, that's Manny's job," I point out.

Emily just shakes her head and rolls her eyes.

"Oh, you were being sarcastic, right?"

With Emily, sometimes it's hard to tell.

I head into my room, flip open my laptop, and shoot off a quick e-mail to Manny.

Hey, Manny.

I just came up with an idea for Sure Things, Inc.'s next invention!

Billy

A few seconds later I get a reply. And this is *so* Manny:

Great! I've got the marketing strategy all planned!

I write back:

But wait, you don't even know what the invention is!

Manny writes back:

Right, right. Whatcha got?

I write back:

The Dog Translator!

I hold my breath waiting for a reply. A few seconds later it comes:

LOVE IT! We'll talk tomorrow.

That's my partner!

Chapter Two

Cats and Dogs

AS IS USUALLY THE CASE WHEN I COME UP WITH AN idea, I sleep poorly that night. I tell myself that I should wait until morning to start thinking this idea through so I can get some sleep.

But, when I'm in the thick of an inventing frenzy, like right now, my brain seems to go on autopilot, tinkering all on its own with the hundreds of tiny details that go into the creation of all of my inventions.

I toss and turn for a few hours, then finally doze off. My dreams are filled with dogs talking to me:

"I'm ready for my walk."
"My bowl is empty! My bowl is empty!"
"Throw the ball. I'm ready! Throw the ball!"

The last image I recall from my dream is Philo saying: *"I love you, Billy,"* then licking my face. I awake to Philo actually licking my face about eleven seconds before my alarm goes off.

"ERRR-RUUFF! RUFF!"

Even without a Dog Translator I know what that means.

"All right, boy, I'll take you out and feed you," I say, dragging my tired bones out of bed.

I shower, get dressed, eat some breakfast, and head off to school—all after taking care of Philo, of course. This whole time I can't get my mind off the Dog Translator. This could be the biggest thing Sure Things, Inc. has ever done. Or could it? I decide to do what Manny would call some INFORMAL, UNOFFICIAL, UNSCIENTIFIC market research. In other words, ask a bunch of kids what they think of my new idea.

As soon as I walk into school, I spot Peter MacHale. When I returned to school after the success of Sure Things, Inc. last summer, Peter was one of the first kids to congratulate me.

"Hi, Peter," I say. "Can I ask you a question?"

"Sure thing, Billy!" he says, a big smile revealing the enormous gap between his two front teeth. "Get it? Sure Thing!"

"Yeah, I get it," I say. "Listen, Peter, you have a dog, right?"

"Sure thing, Billy!" he says again, giggling.

I begin to wonder how many times he's going to make the same joke.

"I have a poodle named Lexi," Peter explains. "Why?"

"How would you like to understand what Lexi is saying every time she barks?" I ask.

"What do you mean?" Peter asks.

"What if there was a device that could translate dog barks into human words?" I ask.

"Cool!" Peter says, seeming genuinely excited. "Do you have one? How much does it cost? Where can I get one?"

"Um, it doesn't exist yet," I explain. "But I am thinking of creating it."

"Sounds like a Sure Thing to me!" says Peter. Then he heads off to class, laughing at his joke a third time.

Well, that's one potential customer.

Next I run into Dudley Dillworthy. Dudley is as tall as a bear standing on the top of Mount Everest. I used to be afraid of him, but it turns out that he's a big fan of the All Ball. Being a famous inventor can have an upside, even in school.

"Hey, Dudley, can I ask you a question?" I

say. I've heard Dudley talk about his dog before.

"What's up, Billy?" he asks. "Invent anything good lately?"

"Uh, a couple of things, but I just want to ask you . . . How'd you like to understand what your dog is saying?" I ask.

"What do you mean?" Dudley asks, scratching his head.

"Like when your dog barks or whines or moans. What if you knew exactly what your dog was trying to say?"

Dudley shrugs. "I never thought about that, but it sounds pretty cool to me."

"Great. Thanks," I say. Then I spot Allison Arnolds at her locker. She's in my math class. A few weeks ago, she was totally *in love* with Dustin Peeler, the singer. But Emily doesn't like him anymore, so maybe Allison doesn't either.

Do you want to know a really BIG SECRET? I kinda maybe sorta think Allison is cute, but I have *never* said anything about it to *anyone*, not even Manny. Especially not Manny. He'd

probably blurt it out at the worst time. He's almost as bad as my dad when it comes to keeping secrets.

"Hi, Allison," I say meekly.

"Hi, Billy," she replies.

She stands there looking at me, waiting for me to say something else. Then I remember why I started talking to her. "So, you have a dog, right?"

"Yeah. I named him Dustin, but I'm thinking of changing his name. 'Dustin' just seems so sixth grade," she says.

"Okay. Well, how would you like to know what what's-his-name is saying?" I ask.

"Who, Dustin Peeler?" she asks.

"No, I mean your dog," I reply.

"Oh, well, I guess so, sure," she says. Then she heads off down the hall.

"Excuse me," I say to a boy I don't know. I figure Manny would want me to include total strangers in my market research. "Would you like it if I invented something to help you understand what dogs are saying?"

"I'd rather you invented something so that I could understand what my *math teacher* is saying," says the boy.

Uh, right. I'll have to file that one away.

I stop several more kids before homeroom. I ask each of them the same question.

"I have a cat," one says. "And a hamster. And a canary. I don't really like dogs."

"I've been waiting for this my whole life! Where can I get one?" says another.

BRIIIIIING!

The bell rings, signaling the end of my research session. Overall, I'd have to say that the majority of people I asked thought that the Dog Translator was a great idea. I'll put it at 84.3 percent in favor. Manny loves it when I use stats like that!

When the school day ends, I launch into my usual routine. I jump on my bike and speed home. Typically it takes me about fifteen minutes to ride from school to home. But on a day like today, when I can't wait to see Manny and start working

84.3%
LOVE
THE DOG
TRANSLATOR

on our next invention, I make it in twelve.

Hurrying around to our backyard, I poke my head into Dad's art studio. He's a painter, and he spends most of his day out here in what is a former garden shed that he's turned into a pretty nice studio—if your definition of "pretty nice" is a paint-splattered shack filled with easels, brushes, and canvases.

Dad is wearing his painting overalls, which he calls his "inspiration apron." This formerly white garment looks like the result of an explosion in the paint section of a hardware store.

"Hey, Dad. I'm home," I say. "Whatcha working on?"

"It's a portrait of Philo," he replies. "I'm trying to capture a sense of what goes on inside his head."

I look over at the canvas. Dad has drawn a pretty good likeness of Philo. He's now adding colors . . . lots of colors that I've never seen on any dog anywhere.

"Cool," I say.

"Off to work?" he asks.

I nod.

"What are you working on today?"

"Let's just say . . . I think you'll like it. And I think Philo will like it too. See ya later for dinner."

"Okeydokey," says Dad.

I dash into the house. Throwing open the fridge, I spy half a peanut butter sandwich leftover from yesterday. I gobble it up, gulp down some milk, and head off in search of Philo.

I take Philo with me to the office every day. I love having him around, and I know he misses me when I'm at school. Philo loves hanging out at the office with Manny and me. He even has his own doggy bed in the corner. Philo is definitely the UNOFFICIAL MASCOT of Sure Things, Inc.

I let out a long whistle. "Phiii-looo," I call.

Philo comes tearing through the house, skidding to a stop at my feet. I lean down and scratch his head. He licks my cheek, and I laugh.

Back outside I hop onto my bike and speed off. Philo trots happily alongside me.

A few minutes later we arrive at Manny's house. I lean my bike against a tree, and Philo and I head to the garage. I can't wait to talk to Manny about the Dog Translator.

I open the door to our office. As soon as I do, **La! La! LaaaH!**, a sound comes blasting out of a speaker hanging just above my head.

It's every ball you'll ever need; the greatest ball you'll own, indeed. No matter what sport you like to play, the All Ball helps you every day. That's all! That's the All Ball!

It's the new jingle for the All Ball! But why is it coming out of this speaker?

Across the room Manny is sitting at his desk. He's having a conversation with someone on his smartphone, messaging someone else on his tablet, and replying to an e-mail on his laptop—all at the same time. Look up the word "MULTITASK" in the dictionary and you'll see Manny's picture.

He turns toward me and puts his hand over his phone.

"You like it?" he calls out. "It's our new doorbell! It'll play every time the door opens. Isn't that great?"

Without waiting for a reply, Manny goes back to his phone call.

Manny loves that jingle. He says he never gets tired of it—maybe that's because he wrote it for our first TV commercial for the All Ball. Me, well, I've heard it plenty of times, and now I have to hear it every time I open the door? We may have to talk about this.

I head inside to my desk, past the soda, pizza, pinball, foosball, and air hockey machines. I squeeze past the basketball hoop and the punching bag. I could go for a custom slice of cherry pie pizza and my very own concoction that I call LIME-PICKLE SODALICIOUS right now, but there's too much work to do. Philo trots over to his doggy bed and curls right up.

"It's simple," Manny says into the phone, "any kid from anywhere in the world can submit any idea to us on our website. The contest is always open and we're always reviewing ideas."

I smile. Manny's talking about Sure Things' Next Big Thing contest. That's how we started manufacturing the Sibling Silencer. It's co-owned with a girl named Abby who came up with the idea. We just helped her create and manufacture it.

But right now the contest will have to be put on hold. The Dog Translator just has to be the next thing we work on.

"Manny, I have to tell you about my idea!" I say. I usually don't like to bother Manny when he's on a call—or three—but I just can't wait to talk about the Dog Translator.

"I'll call you back," Manny says into the smartphone. Then he taps a button on the touch screen. He quickly responds: "Be right back" on his tablet, then hits send on the e-mail he's been writing.

"Yeah, Billy, what's up?" he says, swiveling his chair toward me. "I've just been going through sales figures, and everything is looking up: the All Ball, the Sibling Silencer, the Stink Spectacular, and Disappearing Reappearing Makeup!"

"So what do you think about the Dog Translator for our Next Big Thing?" I ask.

"I love it, but I figured out a way to broaden the scope, as in . . . double the market!" Manny says, smiling. "I did some research. It seems that between 37 and 47 percent of all US households have a dog. That's great. But here comes the broadening-the-scope part—between 30 and 37 percent of all US households have a cat!"

"Yeah," I say cautiously.

"So let's make Sure Things, Inc.'s next great invention . . . the CAT-DOG TRANSLATOR! Whatcha think?"

Before I can answer, Manny continues. "The way I figure it, we can almost double the profits by including cats, allowing us to lower the price and sell more total units."

That's Manny for you, always looking to maximize profits. It's not that Manny cares about money. In fact, the money we make at Sure Things, Inc. usually goes right back into the business . . . or into our college funds. But Manny loves numbers—the bigger, the better. Sometimes I think it's all a game to Manny. And Manny loves games.

Manny is still talking about his big plans. "I figure we start with a stand-alone unit. If that does well, we expand into creating smartphone and tablet apps that can be integrated into—"

"Whoa! Manny, hold on one sec!" I shout.

"What's the matter?" Manny asks, truly puzzled.

"You have failed to take one very important point into consideration," I explain.

"Really?" Manny asks, scratching his head. "What's that?"

"The invention doesn't EXIST yet!" I exclaim.

You know, for a brilliant guy, sometimes Manny misses the most obvious stuff.

"Right, right," Manny says, turning back to his smartphone, tablet, and spreadsheets. "Well, then you better get busy, partner!"

Chapter Three

To the Lab!

I SETTLE INTO MY INVENTOR'S LAB. OKAY, IT'S REALLY a corner of Manny's garage with a workbench, a tool cabinet, a parts cabinet, a bunch of shelves, and a pegboard. Manny calls it the "mad scientist" division of Sure Things, Inc., but that's just because he doesn't understand the type of environment that inventors need to allow our minds to work.

Above my workbench hangs a sign with a quote from my favorite inventor, THOMAS EDISON: "To invent, you need a good imagination and a pile of junk."

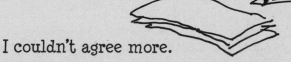

I couldn't agree more.

I admit, it's a little messy. I haven't actually seen the surface of the workbench in a few months. And the cables, wires, plugs, and gizmos dangling from hooks on the pegboard could perhaps be a little more organized. And yes, the last time I needed to find the power drill all I had to do was look in the drawer labeled PRINTER CARTRIDGES.

See? I know where everything is. Just because no one else would have a clue where to find anything . . . well, let's just call that my version of a security system.

I start, as I usually do, with a pencil and a blank piece of paper. Sitting on my official inventor's stool, I quickly sketch out a box in which to hold all the electronics necessary to interpret dog and cat sounds. The device will need a microphone to pick up the sounds, and a speaker so we can hear what the animals are actually saying.

Okay, I have point A and point B all set up. Now I just have to connect those dots. Slipping off my stool, I crawl under my workbench. There I have piles of things I started and never quite got anywhere with.

I find a wooden box in decent shape. That's a good enough start for me. Placing the box on the workbench—or more accurately, shoving aside steel pipes, plastic doll heads, and four roller skate wheels (don't ask!), I set the box on the workbench.

Grabbing my drill—from the printer cartridge drawer—I cut out a large hole in the front of the box. I pick up a curved pipe, which I had just knocked onto the floor, and fit it into the hole.

Now I need wires. Did I mention not to try this at home? Well, don't. Standing on my stool, I look up at a high shelf. There I see a row of boxes. I grab a box of green wires and step down off the stool.

I run about two feet of wire through the pipe and into the box.

Next I need a microphone. I open a drawer in my parts cabinet labeled MICROPHONES (you're shocked, I know) and find a large round microphone.

I connect it to the wire running through the pipe. I'm starting to get a good feeling about this. This just may work.

"Hey, Billy, I already have three major stores interested in the Cat-Dog Translator!" Manny calls out.

Okay . . . so much for my good feeling. Now all I'm feeling is pressure to get this thing done . . . and to get it right.

Next I need a speaker. Since cats and dogs use a variety of sounds and tones rather than actual words, I think an old-fashioned speaker would make it easier to understand the translation.

Back under the workbench for me. I take a stack of blueprints off of an old wooden trunk and place them on the floor. Flipping open the trunk's lid, I rummage around.

Let's see . . . knobs—I could use a couple of those to control the volume . . . buttons, nah . . . dials, and . . . AHA! Speakers!

I pull out a large cone-shaped speaker. It looks like a cross between a megaphone that a cheerleader might use and something people used to use to help them hear.

I drill an even larger hole in the top of the box, then fit the smaller end of the speaker into the hole.

Over the next hour I place knobs, meters, dials, a couple of lightbulbs, and what feels like two miles of wire into the box. Screwing the last knob into place, I step back and look at my creation.

It looks kind of primitive, like something out of an old black-and-white horror movie. Still, my inventor's instinct is that the Cat-Dog Translator needs to be simple and kind of old-fashioned. Anything too sophisticated might go beyond the ability to capture what dogs and cats are saying.

"Make that four major stores, Billy!" Manny shouts across the garage. "I'm on a roll!"

Wonderful. Let's hope that I'm on a roll too! I'm sure this thing will need some tweaks, but the only way to fine-tune it is to test it. Conveniently, we just happen to have a perfect test subject right on the premises.

"Phiii-looo!" I call out.

Philo lifts his head up from his dog bed and stares at me. He looks puzzled. I'm sure he's thinking, *I haven't had time for a full nap. It can't be time to go home already, can it?*

Of course, if this thing works, I'll know exactly what he is thinking.

"Come here, boy!" I call.

Philo just yawns.

Fortunately, I keep a box of doggy treats in my tool cabinet in a drawer labeled DOGGY TREATS.

I pull out the box and shake it. Philo jumps up and trots across the room. All signs of sleepiness VANISH.

I toss a treat into the air. Philo stands up on his back legs and catches it in his mouth. We repeat the process one more time, and then I pick up my rough model of the Cat-Dog Translator.

I hold the microphone portion of the invention up to Philo's mouth.

"Speak, boy!" I say. "Say something."

But Philo just looks up at me, hoping for another treat, and drools. A huge glob of drool splashes down onto the microphone.

Sparks fly from the box. The lightbulbs flash on and off several times, then the whole thing goes dead, making a sickly fizzing sound. A curl of black smoke rises from the box and drifts up toward the ceiling. Philo takes one sniff and trots back to his bed.

"Did you leave some pizza in the machine?" Manny asks without turning around.

"Funny," I say. "Guess I need to add a DROOL GUARD to the microphone portion of this thing. Just think about how much dogs drool."

"Do I have to?" asks Manny.

"No, but I do."

"That's why you're the inventor and I'm the guy who just got a fifth major store interested in the Cat-Dog Translator!" boasts Manny, firing off a text.

As usual, he's so focused on the big picture that the tiny details that make up any invention are lost on him. That's me. The "tiny details" guy. Speaking of which . . . climbing back onto my stool, I reach up to one of my supremely organized shelves for a plastic box labeled PLASTIC STUFF. I pull down the box.

Rummaging through the box I find a square piece of plastic. I hold it up against the microphone and it seems to fit pretty well. At least well enough for a prototype. Using a special bit, I drill a few holes in the plastic. My hope is that the piece will allow the dog and cat sounds in but keep any extraneous drool out. I secure the plastic drool guard to the microphone.

About fifteen minutes later I've replaced all the burned-out wires, circuits, and bulbs. Screwing the box back together, I'm ready for another test.

Grabbing his box of treats, I lure Philo back out of his doggy bed.

"Okay, boy, speak!" I command. "Speak!"

Nothing. Philo always barks at the wrong time. Why can't he bark at the right time?

I hold a treat over my head. "Want it, boy?"

RUUFFF! RUUFFF! barks Philo.

I manage to move the device over to Philo's mouth, just before the second "Ruufff!" A glob of drool bounces off the plastic guard and spatters on the floor. But the machine's lights start flashing.

"I think it's gonna work!" I shout excitedly. "For the first time in human history, we'll actually know what a dog is saying!"

Manny hits save on his laptop and spins his swivel chair around. "This I have to see," he says.

"Or it would be more accurate to say 'hear.'"

The lights stop blinking, and out of the Cat-Dog Translator comes:

"RUUFFF!"

Philo's original bark. Actually, a static-and-feedback-filled, distorted version of his bark.

Without saying a word—because he knows better, even after only being my business partner for a few months—Manny swivels his chair back around to his desk.

I take a deep breath and grab my electric screwdriver. I've been in this situation before. Nothing ever comes that easy. Nothing I invent ever works on the first try. I've got to just keep at it.

"RUUFF! RUFF!" Philo barks.

"Good boy, but I don't need you to bark right now to test the—"

"RUUFFF!" Philo barks even louder.

It's then I remember the treat in my hand.

"Oops. Sorry, buddy. Here you go." I toss the treat into the air, and he snatches it and gobbles it right up.

I open up the box and get back to work tweaking the wiring and the circuits, adjusting my rough blueprints as I go. Before I know it, it's time to head home for dinner. I didn't expect to bang this thing out in one evening anyway. I gather up the prototype and all my drawings and get ready to leave.

"I'm going to have to work this out using the only tried and true inventing method that's ever worked for me," I say.

"SLEEP-INVENTING," says Manny.

"Yup. Sleep-inventing."

Manny slips his laptop, tablet, phone, and a stack of papers into his briefcase. Manny *loves* his briefcase. Even though he's just walking from the garage to the main house, he always carries it. Makes him feel like a BIG-TIME DEAL MAKER, which I guess he is. He follows me to the door.

Suddenly a terrible thought grips me.

"What if I have trouble sleeping?" I ask, becoming genuinely worried. "I mean, the whole future of Sure Things, Inc. depends on my ability to sleep well, but not well enough that I stay in bed all night."

"Maybe you should invent something that helps you sleep, like a helmet that stimulates sleep patterns in the brain," Manny suggests.

"Sure," I say. "No problem. As long as I can invent it before bedtime tonight, we're golden!"

I hop onto my bike and head home, with Philo trotting alongside me—but not before jotting down "SLEEP HELMET" on a piece of paper, which I shove into my pocket.

Chapter Four

are You Talking to Me?

THAT NIGHT, FOLLOWING HOMEWORK, DINNER, and watching my favorite reality TV show: **GIGANTIC FAILS—INVENTIONS THAT WENT NOWHERE!**, a show I hope to never appear on, I go to bed . . .

. . . where I lie on my back, staring at the ceiling, followed by lying on my side and staring at the numbers changing on my clock. I'm usually a pretty good sleeper. It's only been lately, since Manny and I realized that I invent in my sleep, that I have trouble dozing off. Especially when I'm feeling pressure to come up with a new invention.

Finally, after what feels like half the night, I doze off. The next morning I wake with a start, before my alarm even goes off, jump from my bed, and stumble in a sleepy haze over to my desk—where the prototype sits, right next to the rough blueprints I'd brought home the night before. Nothing new. Not even a pencil mark. Clearly I did not get up to sleep-invent last night, and that is not a good thing.

I could use that sleep helmet right about now.

I shower, get dressed, and scramble downstairs for some breakfast, all the time doing my best not to freak out about the fact that I didn't bang out those blueprints in one night.

Emily is waiting at the table. She's wearing glasses. Emily doesn't need glasses. I guess that's her new thing now that she's not talking in a British accent anymore.

"Whatcha workin' on, genius?" she asks, pushing her glasses up on her nose. I can see

that there are no lenses in the frames. "What's the next *brilliant* invention that's going to change the world forever?"

I decide not to say anything about Emily's new accessory. It's best not to engage.

"I'm building a Cat-Dog Translator," I say.

Without changing her expression one bit, between bites of cereal, Emily says: "That's the dumbest thing I've ever heard!"

"Well, thank you for your continued support," I say, shoving an English muffin into my mouth.

Emily just rolls her eyes, which is way more noticeable now that she's got them framed in fake glasses.

I head off to school, where things go about

as well as they've been going everywhere else for the past twenty-four hours, which is to say frustrating.

Peter MacHale stops me in the hall.

"Hi, Billy, seen any talking dogs lately?" he shouts. Then he walks away, laughing.

"Hey, Sure, know what my dog said last night?" asks Dudley Dillworthy.

"No, not really," I reply.

"'BOW-WOW, WOOF-WOOF!'" says Dudley, bursting into laughter, as if he's just said the funniest thing anyone has ever said. "Pretty smart dog, huh, Sure?"

"Pretty smart, yeah," I reply softly.

After school I zip home, grab my bike and Philo, and speed over to Manny's.

I open the front door, completely forgetting about the new "doorbell" he installed:

It's every ball you'll ever need; the greatest ball you'll own, indeed. No matter what sport you like to play, the All Ball helps you every day. That's all! That's the All Ball!

If that jingle rings every time I walk in, I

think I'm just going to crawl through Philo's doggy door.

"I just can't get enough of it," Manny says, humming the jingle's tune. Then he gets right down to business. It's so Manny. "So at lunch you were really worried about how you didn't sleep-invent last night."

I nod. "I might need to invent that sleep helmet so I can sleep-invent again. But then how am I going to invent the sleep helmet if I can't sleep-invent!"

"Slow down, Billy," Manny tells me. "It's just been one night. You'll get it tonight."

Reason #653 why Manny is my best friend and business partner: He always knows just the right thing to say.

I spend the rest of the afternoon making small adjustments to the device, but I hesitate to test it on Philo until I've managed to finish the blueprints.

That night after dinner, instead of watching another episode of *Gigantic Fails*—which, now that I think about it, is probably not the best show for me to watch on a night before I need to invent something—I get into bed with a book: a biography of Thomas Edison.

Maybe it's because I didn't get much sleep last night, or maybe it's because of Manny's reassurance, but tonight I quickly doze off.

"Billy . . ." A soft voice enters my dream. *"Billy, honey, time to get up."*

It's my mom's voice. Actually, it's a recording of my mom's voice, which I programmed into my alarm clock as a nice way to wake me up. She used to wake me up herself every morning, and I miss that now.

My mom isn't around much. She's a scientist who works on TOP-SECRET projects for the government, and so she's often in some far-flung corner of the world. She's been gone since the summer, right after the All Ball made it big. It's nice to hear her voice every morning, but it also reminds me of how much I miss her. I can't wait until she comes home. Until then, we e-mail a lot. In fact, I should make sure to e-mail her today.

Thinking of e-mailing my mom makes me think of my desk, which makes me think of my blueprints. Did I sleep invent last night? Well, there's only one way to find out! I slip from my bed and scoot over to my desk. There, sitting in the middle of my desk, are fully rendered blueprints for Sure Things, Inc.'s Next Big Thing—the Cat-Dog Translator!

Obviously, my good night's sleep included a very productive sleep-inventing session! Rolling up the blueprints, I breathe a little sigh of relief. Now all I have to do is build a working model of the thing.

I have trouble concentrating at school that day. I'm too excited. I can't wait to get to the office and tell Manny the good news. (Manny was busy at lunch, so we hardly saw each other all day.) Finally the afternoon comes, and with Philo at my side, I race to the office.

I'm so excited about the new blueprints that I don't even mind hearing the All Ball jingle again as I slip through the door.

"How'd you sleep?" Manny asks.

"Terribly," I reply, holding up the completed blueprints.

"WONDERFUL!" Manny says. "I knew you'd do it. You are the best!"

It's at moments like this that I remember why Manny and I were best friends long before we became business partners.

Time to get busy! I happily spread the blueprints out on my workbench right next to the prototype. Opening up the prototype's main box, I compare the wiring and circuits inside with the blueprints I drew up last night. I can see right away where I went wrong.

Switching a few connections and adding a few parts from my vast stash of stuff, I do my best to match the blueprints wire for wire, circuit for circuit—each part fitting precisely with all the others.

Finally, after about an hour, I'm ready to test my invention. I power it up. The two lights on top of the translator start blinking—left, right, left, right. A low whirring sound rumbles from the speaker. It's now or never.

Out come the doggy treats.

"Philo! Treat time!" I shout, shaking the box.

Philo hops out of his doggy bed, trots over to me, and sits down. I hold a treat up over his head.

"Speak, boy! Speak!" I say, holding the treat up with one hand, while holding the translator's microphone down near Philo with the other hand.

"RUUFFF! RUFFFF!" he barks. I toss him the treat.

A second later a sound comes out of the

translator's speaker: ". . . ov . . . oo . . ."

Well, it's the closest to a translation that I've gotten to so far, but it's still not precisely right.

I rotate the dials on the front of the device slightly, then repeat the experiment.

"RUUFFF! RUFFFF!" Philo barks again.

This time ". . . love . . . oo . . ." comes out of the speaker.

Closer! Definitely closer!

A few more tweaks on the dials, another doggy treat, and . . .

"RUUFFF! RUFFFF!" Philo is really getting impatient for his treat now.

This time it comes out as: "I LOVE YOU!"

During this whole testing process Manny has been hard at work at his desk with his back to me. He knows enough to leave me alone when I'm in the middle of inventing. But as soon as the "I love you," in a somewhat high, squeaky, yet totally recognizable voice, comes out of the speaker, Manny leaps from his chair, races across the office, and gives me a high five.

"I knew you could do it, Billy!" he cries.

Don't get too excited just yet, I tell my brain. "We still have to make sure it works for cats, too," I point out.

Don't get me wrong. I'm thrilled I've gotten so far, but no invention is complete until everything works the way you want it to. If not, you've just got more work to do.

"Why don't I go get Watson?" says Manny. Watson is Manny's cat. "He usually has to stay in the house, but I can bring him into the garage. Just don't open any doors."

"Great," I reply. "And Philo has always gotten along with cats, so that shouldn't be a problem."

A few minutes later Manny returns carrying a large gray-and-white cat. Watson rests in his arms like a giant furry loaf of bread.

"Okay, kitty, you go say hello to Billy," says Manny, placing Watson on the floor.

Philo is half-asleep in his doggy bed. He lifts his head and sniffs at Watson, who ignores him, walks once around the doggy bed, and then rubs up against Manny's legs.

"Come here, Watson!" I urge the cat.

"Do you have any string?" Manny asks.

Silly question. I pull open a drawer in my parts cabinet labeled jUNK DRAWER #3. I have a total of five junk drawers, plus all my other drawers, which are basically junk drawers too.

Rummaging around among paper clips, rubber bands, and twist ties, I find a length of string. Placing the translator on the floor, I dangle the string near the microphone.

"Come on, Watson, over here!" I call.

Watson spies the bouncing string and darts across the room. As he swats at the string he lets out a loud: **MWOW! MWOOOOW!**

The lights flash, the speakers hum, and out comes: **RUUFFF! RUFFFF!**

"Uh, that sounds like Philo," says Manny.

I always appreciate it when he points out the obvious.

"Hmmm . . . ," I say, scratching my head. "When we decided to make our invention a

Cat-Dog Translator, this is not what I had in mind."

I adjust the dials and slip a sound filter into a slot I had built into the side of the box.

"Let's try this again," I say.

I dangle the string, making it dance right in front of the microphone. Watson grabs it with both paws, then flops over onto his back and moans: "BWaaaRRR!"

From out of the translator's speaker comes: "YOU'RE NOT PETTING ME. IS THERE A PROBLEM?"

Manny jumps so high, his head almost hits the ceiling. He gives me another high five and says, "Another home run, partner! Nicely done!"

"Thanks," I say, breathing a sigh of relief. Another Thomas Edison quote comes to mind: "Genius is 1 percent inspiration and 99 percent perspiration." Not that I'm saying I'm a genius or anything like that. But inventing does takes hard work.

"Thanks, Watson," I say, leaning down and rubbing his belly.

Manny picks up Watson to bring him back into the house.

"I'd like to take Philo and the translator to the park," I say. "You know, kind of field test it out in the 'wild,' so to speak."

"Great idea," says Manny. "Stop back here before you go home and let me know how it works."

I snatch up my backpack and carefully slip the translator inside. "Come on, Philo. You wanna go to the park?" I ask.

At the sound of the word "park" Philo is up and racing to the door. I follow him out and we head to the park, with a working prototype of Sure Things, Inc.'s Next Big Thing!

Chapter Five

Panic in the Park

PHILO TROTS a FEW STEPS aHEAD OF ME aS WE HEAD out through the fence in Manny's backyard and into the park that juts right up to Manny's parents' property. Ever since the success of the All Ball changed my life and I've been coming to Manny's garage every day, this park has been a huge help. I can take a break from work when I need it and make sure Philo gets a quick walk.

Philo jumps up on a bench, then jumps back off and races around the trunk of a thick tree. I set my backpack down and pull out the translator. A few seconds later Philo comes scampering back to me. It makes me smile to see him so happy.

"What's up, boy?" I ask, moving the translator close to him.

"**GRR–RUFFF!**" he barks. Out comes: "I'M HUNGRY!"

"All right, let's get you some food." It's thrilling to be able to understand what it is that Philo wants. Although ninety-nine times out of a hundred, what Philo wants is food.

I toss him a treat, which he catches and gobbles down. Then he happily trots alongside me, sniffing at the ground as he goes. Philo moves closer to me and sniffs near my feet.

"Your feet smell DELICIOUS!" he says through the translator.

Knowing what Philo is saying is both cool and kinda gross at the same time!

We walk a little farther until Philo spots a squirrel dashing through the grass. He stops in his tracks, his tail whipping back and forth, his ears pointing straight up. He begins growling, then barks. What comes out of the translator is: "I'll chase that squirrel . . . NOW!"

Philo bolts after the squirrel, who takes off like a fuzzy gray blur. The squirrel tears through the grass, darting sharply to its left, then cutting back to its right, heading for the edge of the park's large grassy field. Philo matches his moves step for step.

With Philo closing in on him, the squirrel makes for a large tree at the end of the field. Just as Philo is about to catch him, the squirrel reaches the base of the tree and leaps up onto the thick trunk, scrambling up into the high branches, its claws grabbing the craggy bark.

Philo skids to a stop just in time to avoid crashing into the base of the tree. He places his front paws onto the tree and starts barking loudly. I catch up to him in time to use the translator to hear: "PLEASE COME DOWN, SQUIRREL. PLEASE COME DOWN SO I CAN CATCH YOU."

The squirrel probably can't understand what Philo's barks mean, but he certainly gets the point. That squirrel is not budging from its

perch. If the squirrel could, it would probably stick its tongue out at Philo, taunting him. I scratch Philo's head, and he brings his front paws back down to the ground.

"I don't think the squirrel speaks Dog, buddy," I say, realizing, of course, that the Cat-Dog Translator only works one way. I can now understand what Philo is saying, but my words are still just gibberish to him. Now, if I could invent something that would translate human speech into dog language . . . Slow down, Billy. One BRILLIANT INVENTION at a time!

Philo resumes his barking: "I would like to catch that squirrel. Squirrels are fast. Squirrels can climb trees. I also can climb trees."

A strange look comes over Philo's face. As if he has just solved a problem that he's been working on for years, as if a lightbulb has just gone off inside his doggy brain.

"I can climb trees. I can climb trees," he repeats.

Philo looks straight up the tree trunk. But he's too late. The squirrel has disappeared into the highest branches of the tree and is nowhere in sight.

We continue our walk. I decide right then and there to add a long shoulder strap to the Cat-Dog Translator, so that it can hang down near Philo's mouth. That way I won't have to bend down to allow the machine to hear what he's saying.

We pass a garbage can. Philo shoves his nose into the top of the can and sniffs so loudly I can hear it from a few feet away.

"GARBAGE SMELLS DELICIOUS!" he says through the translator. "I'D LIKE SOME GARBAGE, PLEASE."

"Never mind," I say, gently guiding his nose and the rest of him away from the trash can. So far, mostly what I have learned from the Cat-Dog Translator is that Philo thinks just about everything—the more disgusting, the better—smells delicious.

A few minutes later I see someone coming toward us, walking a dog on a leash. Philo spots the dog and starts barking as they pass each other. His barking is loud enough that the translator's microphone picks it up. Out comes: "I WOULD LIKE TO MEET THAT DOG! I WOULD LIKE TO SNIFF THAT DOG'S BUTT!"

The dog walker stops and gives me a pointed look. "Excuse me? What did you just say?"

UH-OH.

"I—um—I didn't say anything," I squeak out and start hurrying away. "I mean . . . Well, it was my . . . well, it's kind of hard to explain, and—um—never mind, have a nice day!"

I think about heading back to the office. The first official field test of the Cat-Dog

Translator has been a great success out in the wild. Except for the whole "causing a stranger to think I was VERY, VERY WEIRD" part. I need to wrap up work for the day and get home with Philo in time for dinner, English homework . . . well, you know the routine.

But at that moment another squirrel darts out right in front of Philo and looks him squarely in the eyes.

Philo cannot resist this obvious challenge. He barks. "I'LL CHASE THIS SQUIRREL—NOW!"' comes out of the translator. The squirrel dashes off, sprinting across the lawn, heading for the nearest tree. Philo takes off after it.

"Philo, come back here!" I shout, slapping my thigh. I really don't have time to chase him down. But Philo is on a mission, and even the thigh slap move doesn't stop him.

Oh great. Now I have to chase him.

I start running after Philo, but carrying the big, bulky translator in my hands really slows me down. I stop, kneel on the grass, and slide the device into my backpack, which I then slip over my shoulders. But by now Philo has quite a lead on me.

I see across the field that the squirrel has reached a tree, jumped onto it, and is climbing quickly up its trunk. This time Philo remembers, in a timely manner, that he, too, knows how to climb trees, although not quite as gracefully as the squirrel.

When I get to the tree, Philo has leaped up onto a low branch and is making his way up, paw by paw, branch by branch. At this point, neither of us can see the squirrel, who has obviously scrambled way up into the tree to safety.

"Come down, Philo!" I shout, now barely able to see him through the leaves. "You lost him, and we have to go home!"

Philo starts to make his way down. His steps are uncertain, and I start to get worried. When he reaches a low branch, he can't seem to figure out how to make it from there back down to the ground.

"Hold on, boy. I'll help you," I say, slipping off my backpack. I place the backpack down on

a nearby bench and turn back to the tree.

"Come on," I say, lifting my arms as high as they can go.

Suddenly, Philo starts growling.

"Oh, be quiet and come down," I say. "I'll help you. Here we go." I stand up on my tippy-toes, stretching my arms to reach him, but Philo continues to growl and bark.

What's he growling about? I wonder. *Maybe he's just scared of jumping down from the tree?*

Finally, after I stretch so far that I think I might be a couple of inches taller than I was when I woke up this morning, Philo jumps down into my arms.

"There you go," I say. "Forget about that dumb squirrel. Let's go and get you some dinner."

But as soon I put him down on the ground, Philo starts growling and barking again.

"What are you trying to tell me, boy?" I ask. "What's got you so worked up?" Then I remember that I've just invented something that can help answer my question. And it's right here in my backpack. "Let's just find out what you're trying to tell me."

I turn to the bench and open my backpack, only to discover that it's EMPTY! The Cat-Dog Translator is GONE!

Chapter Six

Where's Philo?

OKAY. I'M PANICKING. I SEARCH ALL AROUND THE
bench where I set my pack down—under it, on
the grass near it. Nothing.

*Where could the translator have gone? It was only
out of my sight for a minute. Maybe it fell out of my
backpack while I was chasing Philo. If I retrace my
steps, maybe I can find it.*

With Philo at my side, sniffing everything
he passes, I walk slowly back to where I slipped
the device into my pack, retracing my steps,
scouring every inch of the ground.

No sign of the translator.

Could someone have taken it? But how is that possible?

I look down at Philo. "Did you see someone take it? Huh, boy? Is that why you were growling and barking?"

"RaFF–RaFFF!"

Philo's not much help without the translator.

How could someone have lifted it out of my backpack in such a short amount of time—unless whoever took it had been following me, waiting for an opportunity to snatch the device. But who would do that?

I make my way back to the office with Philo.

A few minutes ago I was thrilled with how well the Cat-Dog Translator worked. Now I not only have to tell Manny that it's gone, but that someone may have stolen it. We'll have to figure out who . . . and why . . . and where it is . . . and how to get it back!

All right, I have to calm down.

I arrive at the garage and throw open the front door, bracing myself for the dreaded All Ball jingle doorbell. It doesn't come. Could Manny have actually taken the fact that I was sick of hearing it to heart? Could he have put aside his pride in having written it? Did he turn it off as a gesture toward harmony in our office?

Nah, must be a short in the audio system.

"No, I don't believe that it will work on hamsters," I hear Manny say as I step into the room. He turns toward me and hits the mute button on his phone.

"It doesn't work on hamsters, right?" he asks me.

I shrug. "Well, I really can't tell without testing it."

Who thought we liked to run around in circles?

Manny nods and hits the mute button again.

"Good news. The hamster setting is in the testing phase," he lies. "What? Fish? Fish don't make any noise. Listen, I'll be in touch when we get the hamster thing up and running."

Manny ends his call. "That was someone from Pet-A-Palooza, the pet store giant. They've got stores in malls all across the country. And they are very, very interested in the Cat-Dog Translator. Hmm . . . we may have to change the name if it works on hamsters, too. CAT-DOG-HAMSTER TRANSLATOR is a bit of a mouthful. Do you think a hamster setting can be integrated into the device?"

"Maybe," I reply. "Of course, that would require us to actually have the device in our possession."

"What do you mean?" Manny asks.

"Someone stole it."

Manny remains calm. In fact, Manny always remain calm. It's reason #207 why he's the best CFO a kid entrepreneur could ask for. It's one of the reasons we became friends, and it is certainly a big reason why Sure Things, Inc. has been such a success. Well, that and the inventions, of course.

"How did that happen?" Manny asks.

"It was only out of my sight for a minute . . . maybe less," I explain. "I think someone was following me and planned to steal it. When Philo got stuck in a tree—"

"Wait? Philo got stuck in a tree?" Manny asks.

"Yeah. That doesn't matter now. What matters is that I put the translator in my backpack, and then I put the backpack down so I could help Philo get out of the tree. When I picked my backpack up again, it was empty."

Manny thinks for a moment, then turns back to his desk. "Hey, I started working on the press release for the Cat-Dog Translator. It's just a rough draft, but tell me what you think:

Wonder what your dog is asking for when he barks at you?

Curious about why your cat paces from one end of the house to the other, moaning?

Well, wonder no more:

Sure Things, Inc., the company that brought you the All Ball, the Sibling Silencer, the Stink Spectacular, and Disappearing Reappearing Makeup, announces their latest, greatest invention:

THE CAT-DOG TRANSLATOR!

Coming soon to a pet store near you!

"We may have to tweak it if the hamster thing works out. Hamsters squeak, right?" asks Manny.

"It's a great press release, Manny, but the device is gone and we have no idea where it is. What are we supposed to do?"

"Build another prototype," Manny says casually, and then he turns his attention back to his press release.

"That's it? Just build another prototype? Just like that?"

"Uh-huh," Manny replies. "Because let's be honest, Billy. You're not the most organized person. I'm sure it'll turn up eventually."

It takes a moment to sink in, but I slowly realize that Manny is right. We have to have a prototype if we're going to demonstrate this thing and make it a hit. And as for what happened to the first prototype, it could have been some kind a prank. Like Manny says, maybe it'll turn up.

"Right!" I announce, as much to get myself psyched as to let Manny know that I agree with his plan. "I'll get on it first thing tomorrow. I have to get home now. See ya."

"Which sounds better: 'LATEST, GREATEST INVENTION' or 'GREATEST, LATEST INVENTION'?"

"Good night, Manny," I say, heading for the door. "Come on, Philo. Let's go home."

That night, as I try to fall asleep, my brain is going a trillion miles a minute. It will take me a couple of days to build a new prototype from scratch. The good news is that I'll be starting with my completed blueprint, so this second model should work even better than the first one. But part of me can't stop worrying that the theft of the first prototype might have been more than just a simple prank.

On Saturday, with Philo at my side, I head to the office. As usual, Manny is hard at work at his desk.

"I definitely like 'latest, greatest invention' better than 'greatest, latest invention.' We should go with that," he says.

Sometimes Manny forgets about stuff like "hello" and "how are you?" But that's okay. He's got bigger things on his mind.

"Did you go to bed last night?" I ask, worried that he will burn himself out. "Have you been here all night fretting over 'latest' and 'greatest'?"

"Nah, I solved that one yesterday," Manny explains, tapping away on his laptop's keyboard. "I just wanted to let you know what I decided."

I slide over to my workbench, unroll the blueprints, and get to work on the Cat-Dog Translator prototype, take two. Philo curls up in his doggy bed.

An hour later I've got the box built. As I go about connecting the wires and circuits, Philo gets up and comes over to me. I don't need a translator to know what that means. He wants to go out for our daily stroll in the park.

I enjoy our walks too, as a short break in my workday. But today I'm trying to get this second prototype built in time for Manny to show it to all the big shots he's lining up.

"Sorry, buddy, no walk today," I say. "But you can go out into the backyard. Come on."

Philo follows me to the door. I open it and he runs out. He'll stay out there for a while, then come scratching at the door so I can let him back in. We've done this before. And with the fence enclosing Manny's backyard, I can send him outside and he's nice and safe.

I dive back into my work. An hour later, with the wiring done and the piping for the microphone and speaker in place, I decide to call it quits for the day. I should be able to wrap this up tomorrow and put Sure Things, Inc. back on track.

That's when I realize that Philo never came scratching at the door.

I get up and step out into the backyard, but there is no sign of him.

"Philo!" I call. Nothing. "Here, boy!" I shout. No Philo.

Where could he have gone?

I walk to the far end of the yard and see doggy paw prints in the dirt. It appears that Philo has jumped the fence! But why would he do that? More importantly . . . where is he?

I stick my head back into the office. "Philo's missing," I tell Manny. "I'm off to search for him. He's probably in the park."

Manny types away furiously. I'm not sure if he even knows I'm in the room.

"Try the park," he says, without breaking his tappity-tappity rhythm on the keyboard. It's like he never even heard me.

"Good idea," I say, then I head back out.

Leaving through the gate at the back of the yard, I walk into the park. As I enter, I look around on the ground, still hoping that I might find the first prototype. No such luck, of course.

"Philo!" I shout. "Here, boy!"

A few seconds later Philo comes bursting out of a clump of nearby bushes.

"**aRRUFFF!**" he barks.

"What's gotten into you?" I say. "How did you get out of Manny's backyard? Did you jump over the fence?"

"**aRRRRRR!**"

Uh-huh, I think. *Where's my prototype when I need it?*

Soon Philo and I are back in the office.

"Found him!" I announce.

By this time Manny has finished what he was doing. "He must have jumped the fence," Manny says. "Good thing the park is fully enclosed with a higher fence. Philo isn't going anywhere farther."

"It's still strange behavior for him, though," I point out. "Anyway, we're heading home. See you tomorrow, Manny."

"Hey, how's this: 'the latest *and* greatest invention'? What do you think? I like the 'and.'"

"Good night, Manny," I say, heading out with Philo by my side.

The next afternoon at the office the same thing happens with Philo. I let him out into the backyard. Making the final connections for the microphone and speaker, I complete the second prototype. Time to test it. And that's when I realize that Philo never came back and scratched at the door to be let in. Just like yesterday.

Again, I head to the park, and again I call out for Philo.

"Here, boy!" I shout.

Philo comes tearing out of the same clump of bushes as the day before.

"What could be so interesting in those

bushes that you jumped the fence and came here two days in a row?" I ask Philo.

He sniffs the ground and remains silent.

I walk over to the bushes and shove the branches aside, not exactly sure what I'm expecting to find there, other than some kind of answer. Maybe the first prototype? But there's nothing interesting about these bushes. There's just dirt and grass and twigs and a startled bird that flies away.

"Come on, Philo. Let's go back," I say.

A few minutes later, back in the office, I decide to test out my new prototype on Philo, hoping to learn why he's been sneaking off to the park.

Powering up the device, I hold it near Philo's mouth.

"Why have you been jumping the fence and going to the park?" I ask.

"GRRRRRR-UFFF!" Philo replies. A few seconds later from the translator's speaker comes: **"TREATS ARE DELICIOUS!"**

So much for getting the truth out of Philo!

Chapter Seven

Sure Secrets!

ON MONDAY MORNING, I JUMP FROM BED, ENERGIZED by the completion of the second translator prototype. Now we're ready for the testing and marketing phase, something I always enjoy. It helps me grasp the fact that all this is real—the inventions, Sure Things, Inc., this double life I'm leading. The thought of another hit invention is enough to get me through even the toughest day at school—usually. But nothing could prepare me for what happens as soon as I walk through the front door.

As I walk down the hall on the way to

homeroom, it seems as if everyone is pointing at me and smirking, or hiding a giggle, or whispering into the ear of the person standing next to her.

Now, by this time I'm somewhat used to being the center of attention—I don't like it, but I am getting used to it. But today's reaction to me seems just plain weird.

Peter MacHale comes up from behind, taps me on the shoulder, and says: "Hey, Sure, you still wear footie pajamas?"

Uh . . . WHAT? I am so stunned by this out-of-left-field comment that by the time I can pick up what little is left of my wits off the floor, Peter has disappeared down the hallway—though I think I can still hear the nasal snort that passes for his laugh.

And for the record, what's wrong with wearing pajamas with feet? They're way warmer than regular ones, and it's not like I wear them to school or anything. I've never noticed a label on them that that says: "If you are twelve and still wearing these, then you are officially super totally lame."

But here's the main thing. How in the world could Peter MacHale know what I wear at home?

Footie pajamas are warm.

As I ponder this new mystery, Dudley Dillworthy waves at me from across the hall. "Hey, Billy, I heard that you talk in your sleep," he shouts, loud enough for everyone in the entire school to hear him. "What do you talk about? Do you count all the money you make from your inventions instead of counting sheep? One million, two million. Ha-ha-ha!"

And again, mocking laughter trails away down the hall. What Dudley said is just as true as what Peter said. I do talk in my sleep. But why would he know that? And why would he care?

"Jelly beans on pizza, Billy?" says a girl behind me.

I know that voice without even turning around. It's ALLISON ARNOLDS.

"Hi, Allison. What was that?" I ask, hoping that I didn't just hear what I'm sure I just heard.

"I asked if you really put jelly beans on your pizza?" she says. "You are just too weird."

Then she walks away.

Again, what she said is true, but who cares what I like to eat? But that's not the real problem. The only one who's ever seen me eat jelly beans on pizza is Manny, and he's certainly not going around blabbing with anybody about stuff that goes at the office. When it comes to the goings-on at Sure Things, Inc., everything, right down to the jelly beans, is top secret to Manny.

So how can all these people know about stuff that happens when it's only me or when it's just Manny and me at the office?

And I thought this was going to be an okay day!

After school I pick up Philo and head to the office. Manny's math class took a field trip to a museum today, so he missed hearing about all the fun I had to endure.

"You are never going to believe what happened to me at school today," I say to Manny, who is deeply absorbed in some website on his laptop. "Peter MacHale made fun of me for wearing footie pajamas, and then Allison Arnolds told me she thinks I'm weird because I like jelly beans on my pizza."

"Uh-huh," Manny mumbles, still riveted to whatever website he's stuck on.

"How do they know these things about me?" I continue. "I didn't tell them. You certainly didn't tell them."

"No, I didn't," says Manny, finally acknowledging the fact that we are having a conversation. "But someone else did. Look." He points to his laptop's screen.

I lean over Manny's shoulder. Pulled up on the screen is a website called SURE SECRETS! EVERYTHING YOU EVER WANTED TO KNOW ABOUT KID INVENTOR BILLY SURE.

I'm stunned. I'm speechless. I don't even know where to begin to start to think about what to say. Fortunately, Manny sees this and picks up the conversation for us both.

"You know I have a bunch of web alerts that let me know anytime Sure Things, Inc. is mentioned?" Manny begins.

I nod weakly, but I am not ready to actually utter a sentence.

"Well, this website popped up in my alerts late last night," he explained. "But I didn't need an alert to find out about it. It's all anyone could talk about during the field trip today."

Words finally return to my frozen lips. "Who would do such a thing?" I ask.

"There's more. Look," says Manny.

Looking past today's three "headlines," which just happened to be about footie pajamas, talking in my sleep, and eating jelly beans on my pizza, Manny finds a longer list of Sure Secrets.

Billy Sure sings in the shower. (Who doesn't?)

Billy Sure turns his socks inside out and wears them two days in a row. (So, they're a little stinky. It saves me from running out of socks.)

Billy Sure won't eat purple candies. (That's true. Not even purple jelly beans.)

Billy Sure hides his spinach under his napkin and then throws it in the garbage when no one is looking.

"I really don't like spinach," I explain

spinach hidden here!

to Manny calmly, as if I were reading these things about someone else. Then the truth that someone is posting these things about me comes crashing down on my brain once again.

"It's a really junky website," says Manny, as if that's supposed to make me feel better. It doesn't.

"Who is doing this? And where is the info coming from? And most importantly, why is someone trying to embarrass me like this?"

"I dug around to see if I could penetrate the site's code," says Manny, "but all I found was a pop-up ad for DON'T-SMELL-LIKE-POO shampoo. I couldn't see who created it. "

"Thanks," I say, back at my workbench.

As I hook up electric meters, voltage measuring devices, and all the other testing tools I use to put every new invention through its paces, I find it hard to concentrate on the work at hand.

Philo gets up and stands at the back door, wagging his tail. Without thinking about it, I get up and let him out.

Time to concentrate, I think. *There's nothing you can do to fix this problem right now.*

The good news of the day is that the

technical testing of the Cat-Dog Translator all goes smoothly. It's time to try it out on other cats and dogs.

When it's time to go home, there is no sign of Philo in the backyard. This is starting to become a pattern. I slip through the gate, walk to the park, and call out.

"Philo! Time to go home!"

Like clockwork, he comes out of the bushes, barking happily and wagging his tail.

When I get home I go right to Emily's room. I knock on her door.

"Yeah!" she calls out.

"Emily, it's me," I say.

"Really?" she says, her sarcastic tone turned up to eleven.

"Can I come in for second?"

"If you must," she replies.

Emily is at her desk, typing furiously on her laptop. She has three history books open and two encyclopedia websites up. She is still wearing her fake glasses.

At that moment I realize that I almost

never see my sister working so hard. She's usually on her phone with three friends at once, fussing with her hair or nails, squealing about the latest bit of gossip. Somehow the sight of EMILY THE SERIOUS STUDENT catches me off guard.

"What?" she snaps.

"Look, I know you're busy, but I need to show you this website," I explain.

She must see how really upset I am, because she saves her work and turns the keyboard over to me.

I bring up the Sure Secrets website, and her mouth drops open.

"What is this?" she asks, scanning the headlines. "Jelly beans? Really? Is that true, because if it is, it's kinda disgusting."

"Yes, it's true, but that's not the point," I say taking a deep breath. "There is all kinds of stuff on this website that is true, but that no one else could possibly know. So I have to ask you, did you do this? Did you tell anyone all this embarrassing stuff about me?"

I brace myself for the confession I am certain will follow, but once again, Emily surprises me.

"No," she says seriously. "I would never do this to you. I mean, I think you're a dork and all, and sometimes I wish you lived in another house, or planet, but I would never do anything like this, Billy."

I know she is telling the truth. Ever since I invented the Disappearing Reappearing Makeup for her, we've been on pretty good terms.

"I know. Thanks. But what about Dad?" I ask.

"Dad?" she repeats. "I don't think Dad has left his studio in a week. The only people he's talked to are me, you, and Philo. And I don't think Philo's talking!"

Not without the Cat-Dog Translator, anyway, I think.

"Thanks, Em," I say.

"Sure. Now get out of my room, genius," Emily snaps, but I can tell that she isn't really annoyed with me. "Can't you see I have mounds of homework to do?"

I head down the hall to my room to begin my own homework, determined to put this website business out of my mind. After all, who cares if everyone knows that I wear footie pajamas or talk in my sleep? So what? Besides, I have more important things to focus on. It's time to move forward with the launch of Sure Things, Inc.'s latest invention!

Chapter Eight

Talking Pets

THE NEXT DAY AS I WALK INTO SCHOOL I BRACE myself for another round of people laughing at me because of stuff they saw on the Sure Secrets website.

I hurry along, keeping my head down, hoping to scoot into class without anyone stopping me in the hallway. No such luck.

"Hey, Sure!" Dudley shouts at me from down the hall.

Here it comes, some embarrassing secret about what I eat or wear or how I sleep. Soon I'm not going to have any secrets left. But much to my shock, Dudley has something else in mind entirely.

"So I heard that you actually invented that dog-talking thing," he says.

"The Cat-Dog Translator, yes, I did actually build one," I say, relieved that the topic of hallway conversation has shifted from my secrets to my work.

"Yeah, whatever, the thing that tells you what your dog is saying," Dudley goes on. "Can I come over and try it on my dog?"

I suppose that's not the worst idea. I do need to test the device. Before I can respond, a crowd forms around me. Some of the kids I know, many I don't.

"You're Billy Sure, right?" says one boy. "Can you try your machine on my cat? I've always wanted to know what he's saying when he yowls at me."

"Well, I think that's possible if I—"

"Billy, I think my dog is really smart," says a girl I don't know. "He always knows what I'm saying, but I'd love to know what *he's* saying."

93

"We might be able to—"

"My cat never shuts up. What the heck is she saying?" says a sixth grader. I think his name is Tommy.

"Hey, I have a gerbil. Will your toy work on him?" says another sixth grader, also named Tommy.

"Um, it's not a toy, actually, it's an—"

"I have a goldfish!"

"Goldfish can't talk!"

"My dog can talk. He never shuts up!"

This is really getting out of control. I mean, on one hand, I do need test subjects, and it seems as though I've got plenty. On the other hand, I have to be able to walk down the hallway in school without creating a scene.

"Okay!" I shout. "Listen up, everyone. Bring your pets to the offices of Sure Things, Inc. this afternoon, and I can test the Cat-Dog Translator on them."

I turn to try to break away from the crowd—and crash right into PRINCIPAL GILAMON.

"Whoa, easy there, Billy," he says, steadying

me so I don't either fall on the floor or knock him over. Knocking over the principal is never a good idea. "Everything okay here? Am I late for this meeting of the Billy Sure Fan Club?"

"No, sir," I say. "I'm just talking with a few friends, but now I'm on my way to class."

"All right, then," says Principal Gilamon as the crowd breaks up. "And perhaps it's time to start thinking about Billy Sure Day again. You, young man, continue to be an inspiration, a model for hard work, and I want the whole school to celebrate that!"

"Thank you, sir. Maybe we could talk about Billy Sure Day another time. It's just that I've been kinda busy and—"

"Well, when you're ready, you just let me know and we'll arrange it," says Principal Gilamon.

"I will. Thank you," I say, hurrying off in the direction of my first class.

Since the first day of seventh grade, Principal Gilamon has been trying to get me to lead a school assembly. Something about my achievements setting off a tidal wave of excellence throughout the school, or some such thing.

Whatever. At least he got me away from the overenthusiastic crowd of pet lovers who had me trapped in the hall.

The rest of the school day follows a similar pattern as the morning. Apparently word of my invention has spread like Principal Gilamon's TIDAL WAVE, and I am mobbed in the hallway between every class by kids wanting to know what their pets are saying.

Finally, the school day ends, and I make my escape. I head home, grab Philo and a peanut butter sandwich, and bike over to Manny's. The

sight awaiting me there is almost too much for me to take in.

As I roll to a stop on my bike, I see a line of kids and pets stretching around the block. Word has obviously spread, not only about the existence of the prototype, but also of my offer to test it on any pet brought to the office.

I wonder how Manny is dealing with all this! Are his parents going to kick us out of our office?

"Hey, Sure. Fluffy's ready to be tested!"

"No fair. I was here first. He cut the line!"

The crowd is starting to get worked up. I slip into the office.

"Have you seen what's going on outside?" I ask Manny.

He's hunched over his laptop, spreadsheets and pie charts flashing across the monitor.

"What? Is it raining or something?" he asks distractedly. "I've been busy working on the marketing plan for the mass launch of the Cat-Dog Translator. Once the beta testing is done I want to go wide with this one, Billy."

"*Raining?!*" I cry. "Have you taken a look out the window? There's, like, a hundred kids out there. And they all want me to test the translator on their pets!"

Manny looks up from his laptop. "That's fantastic!" he says. "Sounds to me like you've got the entire beta test lined up right here!"

I hadn't thought of it that way. As usual, Manny has found the silver lining. I only hope his neighbors agree.

I go to the front door and throw it open.

"Okay, everyone, come in one at a time, and we'll test the Sure Things, Inc. Cat-Dog Translator on your pet," I announce.

First in is a girl named Sara with a small white fuzzy dog. She carries the dog in her arms. As she enters, the dog lets out a tiny yelp.

Philo lifts his head from his doggy bed, surveys the situation, and then puts his head back down on his paws.

I power up the translator. The lights on top flash, left, then right. A low hum comes from the speaker.

"This is my dog, Marshmallow," says Sara.

"Okay," I say, "just put your dog's mouth over near the microphone, right here." I point to the square box extending from the front of the device.

The girl extends her arms so that her dog's mouth is now near the microphone.

"YIP-YIP-YIP-YIP!" the little dog squeaks. From out of the speaker comes: "SARA SMELLS LIKE LIVER . . . YUMMY!"

"I do not!" Sara shrieks, moving Marshmallow away from the device. "I hate liver!" She leaves.

Next in is Dan, with his cat, Boots, a big black cat with white paws.

"I love you, Boots," says Dan, scratching the cat between the ears.

"ME-OOOOW!" cries Boots, who then turns around and lifts his tail. From the translator's speaker comes: "TALK TO THE TAIL!"

Melissa brings in her dog, Hercules. He's a big bulldog. He looks like a Hercules.

"Go ahead, Hercules. Speak!" Melissa says.

"**RaRRRFFFF!**" barks Hercules, practically shaking the walls of the garage. Out comes: "'I LOVE YOU . . . AND YOU . . . AND YOU . . .'"

Sometimes the toughest-looking pets are actually the sweetest.

Herman Torosian comes in carrying a tiny cat carrier. I've seen Herman around school. He's on the football team. He's in eighth grade, but I think he's already taller than my dad. I have to stifle a laugh when he takes a tiny kitten out of the carrier. Standing in the palm of Herman's enormous hand, the kitten meows. She's saying: "SCRATCH MY HEAD. . . . SCRATCH MY HEAD. . . . SCRATCH MY HEAD!"

Herman obliges, though his thumb is almost bigger than the kitten's entire head.

Mary Jane Murphy brings in Killer, her rather large gray cat. She places Killer on the floor, and the cat immediately rolls over onto her back and starts purring loudly. Out of the translator comes: "SCRATCH MY BELLY." Mary Jane starts scratching Killer's belly. "THAT FEELS GOOD. . . . SCRATCH THERE. . . . THAT FEELS GOOD. . . . NOW I HAVE TO BITE YOU!"

Which Killer does . . . but gently.

The PARADE OF PETS continues for hours. In addition to a bunch of dogs and cats, kids also bring in their guinea pigs, birds, hamsters, and turtles. Much to their disappointment—but not mine—the translator doesn't work on any animals other than cats and dogs.

Finally, the last pet comes through and is successfully translated. I'm exhausted. I don't know how Manny can get any work done with the racket in here, but I have to go home.

"Sorry about all the noise," I say.

"Huh, what noise?" Manny asks.

I smile. I have to hand it to Manny. I've never known anyone who can concentrate so completely on what he is doing, no matter what else is going on all around him.

"The good news is that the beta test is a rousing success," I say.

This gets Manny's attention. "Fantastic,"

he says. "I'm putting the final touches on the marketing plan. We are good to go!"

Dinner with Emily and Dad that night is fairly quiet.

"Any progress on figuring out who put up that website?" Emily asks, when Dad heads into the kitchen to get the big bowl of spaghetti he's made. As usual the spaghetti will be mostly inedible. Dad says he added beets, anchovies, and asparagus to the sauce.

"Not yet," I say, realizing that with all the hubbub around testing the translator, I had not thought about the Sure Secrets website once that night.

"Who's hungry for spaghetti?" announces Dad, placing the steaming bowl on the table. "Come and spa-GET-y it!"

Emily rolls her eyes. I actually think it's kinda funny. I'd smile if I wasn't grimacing from the smell of Dad's concoction.

"How's that new invention coming along?" Dad asks.

"It's actually working out really well," I

explain proudly. "Today I tested it at the office, and—"

Suddenly a huge commotion breaks out just outside our window. People are yelling. Cats and dogs are howling.

"What is going on out there?" asks Dad.

Fearing the worst, I jump up from the table and race to the window. Pulling aside the curtain, I see a crowd of kids gathered outside our house. Each one has AT LEAST one pet!

Who can ruin spaghetti? My Dad!

Chapter Nine

More Secrets, More Problems

OBVIOUSLY, WORD ABOUT THE PROTOTYPE HAS GOTTEN out! And it seems that it's gotten out to everyone in the neighborhood.

Staring out the window I see a scene of total pandemonium. Cats scurry up trees. Hamsters dig holes in the lawn. A ferret chases a puppy.

Dad may be a terrible cook, but he's an excellent gardener. He's responsible for how nice our yard always looks. At the moment a very large Saint Bernard has one of Dad's prize-winning rose bushes dangling from its mouth.

Then a horse decides that our driveway is a perfect spot to leave us a present. Guess who's going to have to clean up after him?

"What's going on out there, Billy?" Dad asks. "Does this have something to do with your new invention?"

"It does, and I'll take care of it, Dad!" I say.

I head up to my room to grab the prototype, but not before Emily goes to the window and I hear her say: "Billy, what have you done! There's a CIRCUS on what used to be our front lawn! And in the driveway, there's . . . there's . . . What is that? It's . . . oh no. . . ."

I hurry into my room and throw open the window.

"Hello, everyone," I shout.

I'm greeted by a chorus of overly excited pet owners:

"I wanna know what my pigeon is saying!"

"My dog is really smart. I need to know if he understands me!"

"I just have to know which cat food my Muffy prefers!"

This is nuts. There's no way I can meet with each one of these people and translate what the pets are saying. I'd be out in the front yard all night. I've still got homework to finish, not to mention cleaning up after the horse!

I have an idea. I grab the prototype and quickly adjust the long-range settings on the microphone and the speaker so that they will both work at a distance. I go back to the window.

"Quiet, please, everyone," I shout. "Quiet. In a moment I am going to turn on the Sure Things, Inc. Cat-Dog Translator. It should work for all of you with a cat or a dog, so please listen closely to discover what your pet is saying."

I hold the device up to the open window and power it on.

The cacophony of animal noises drifts into

the microphone and back out the speaker, translated, all at the same time. The symphony of sound is very confusing, but at the same time, pretty awesome:

"Time for a walk. . . . I like walks. . . . Time for a walk. . . . I like walks."

"Treat-treat-treat-treat-treat-treat-treat!"

"Why is there another cat here? I'm the cat! I'm the cat! She knows that I'm the cat!"

"I don't see my ball. Where's my ball? Did you throw the ball? You always throw the ball. Where's my ball?"

This crazy scene goes on for about five minutes. In addition to the pet owners, my poor neighbors have gathered in front of their houses to see what in the world this racket is about. Then I turn off the translator.

"Thank you all for coming," I shout. "The demonstration is now officially over!"

"But Muffy never told me which food she prefers!"

"We will be on the market with the product soon!" I shout. Then I close my window.

Slowly, the crowd breaks up. I venture downstairs. Dad is in the kitchen, obliviously doing the dishes. Emily is in the living room, texting. Everything seems normal.

"Zoo time all done?" she asks without taking her eyes off her phone.

"Yeah, all except for the cleanup," I say, sighing.

I head outside. The crowd is gone, and the neighbors are back in their houses. Grabbing a shovel from the garage, I fill in the holes in the lawn, then replant Dad's rose bush. Unspooling the hose, I head to the driveway to get rid of the evidence of that horse.

The next day at the office I'm exhausted. Between the line-up of people at the office wanting to test out the translator, the mob scene at my house last night, not to mention the Sure Secrets website postings, and Philo's daily journeys to the park, I'm wiped out. Oddly enough, despite his unsupervised running around, Philo has actually been gaining weight lately. Yet one more unexplained piece of this puzzle.

"I don't know, Manny, I know that the Cat-Dog Translator is a good thing, but all this stress is starting to wear me down," I explain. "I had a ton of people show up at my house last night, all with their pets. And not just cats and dogs! There were ferrets and horses, and—"

"Well, here's some good news to help cheer you up," Manny says. "I just completed a deal with YUMMY IN THE TUMMY."

"Yummy in the Tummy? The big pet food company?" I ask. "Really?"

"Really!" Manny says proudly. "They have agreed to endorse and help promote the Cat-Dog Translator. And to show their interest, they have sent us a big fat check to seal the deal. This nice chunk of cash will help fund the manufacturing of the product for the mass market. Now that the prototype

is a success, we can move right into the mass-production phase. We could have this PUPPY on the shelves by the end of the year!" Manny laughs at his little joke.

I lean back in my chair. It's at moments like this that all the craziness seems worth it. The hard work, school, the double life, all of it, have come together to create something successful. I feel proud of my work, and of Manny. I feel happier than I have in days.

Which is exactly when I hear Manny say, "Uh-oh."

"Uh-oh" is something that you definitely do *not* want to ever hear Manny say. He is so calm, and not much ever flusters him, so an "uh-oh" from Manny is like a "HOLY COW! WHAT IN THE WORLD IS GOING ON!" from anybody else.

I walk over to Manny's desk, bracing myself for the worst . . . which is exactly what I get. Manny has the Sure Secrets website up on his computer.

"It looks like the posts are getting more

intense. You're not going to like this one," he says.

"Let me see," I say, leaning in close. "'Billy Sure has a crush on Allison Arnolds!'" I read aloud.

I can feel my face start to blush.

Manny turns and looks up at me. "You do?" he asks. "You really have a crush on Allison Arnolds? Why didn't you ever tell me?"

"I never told anyone!" I reply, a bit more loudly than I would like. "I mean, I might have said it when I was alone in my room with Philo, just to see how it sounded, but I never told anyone."

Manny says nothing as he clicks through the site. I'm watching his face rather than the monitor. That's how I see his startled expression.

"What now?" I ask.

"Um, I think that this is the most serious post so far," Manny says softly.

"'Billy's mother has been away from home a lot lately,'" Manny reads. "'Everyone in the house misses her, but no one talks about where she is or what she is doing. What SECRET things could she be up to?'"

I have to step away from the computer for a moment. Manny is right. This is the worst post so far. It's enough to spill *my* secrets, but my mom should be left out of it . . . especially because I've often wondered what she's really up to too. Manny thinks she's a spy, and I'm beginning to wonder about that myself. All the more reason her secrets shouldn't be posted on a website.

I turn back to Manny. "Enough is enough," I pronounce. "This has gone on long enough. Time to put a stop to this!"

Chapter Ten

Pet Peeves

THE NEXT DAY, JUST OUTSIDE THE SCHOOL, MY TWO problems confront me at the same time.

"Hey, Sure!" shouts Douglas Braintree. "Is it true that your mom has been away for a long time and nobody knows what she does?"

"No, actually," I begin, wondering why my family's personal business is anyone else's business too. "She's a scientist."

"Yeah, right," sneers Douglas. "That's a great cover story. What does she really do, Sure? Is she a secret agent? A government spy? Come on, you can tell me."

I have no idea what in the world gives Douglas Braintree—who I've maybe spoken five words to in all the years we've been in the same school—the idea that I could trust him with any important information, much less with details about my family.

"Yeah, Douglas, that's it," I say, really getting tired of all this. "Her real name is JANE BOND."

As soon as I enter the building, I hear laughter coming from a group of girls.

"You have a crush on Allison Arnolds?" asks Petula Brown, giggling behind the stack of books she holds in her arms.

Oh no. This is it. I'm doomed!

"Where'd you hear that?" I ask. "Did she say something to you?"

"No! I don't talk to Allison Arnolds," says Petula, using a tone that suggests that I'm the dumbest thing ever to walk on two legs. "Not after what happened with Peter MacHale at the Spring Dance last year."

"No, of course not," I say, trying to sound

like I have any idea what she is talking about. "So, you saw that website?"

"Who hasn't?" says Petula, rolling her eyes.

"Well, do you know if Allison has seen it?" I ask.

"And how exactly would I know that?" she asks, growing more exasperated with each word she says. "I just told you I don't talk to her. Remember?"

Tossing her long red hair over her shoulder, Petula walks away without waiting for a response, which I was not about to give her anyway.

Manny and I simply have to figure out who put the site up and how we can take it down, or my life is going to be over. I'm embarrassed that the whole world knows that I like Allison, but there could be worse secrets that could be revealed, and that's exactly what I want to avoid.

As I make my way to my locker, Brian Josephs, a kid from my science class, comes up to me.

"So, I heard that lots of people brought their pets to your house last night?" he says, reminding me that he is one of those people who makes everything he says sound like a question, whether it is or isn't.

"Yeah, that's true," I reply.

"And that all the pets talked at once?"

"Uh-huh."

"And then everything they said got translated by your toy?"

"Well, it's actually not a toy, it's an—"

"And that it was REALLY, REALLY LOUD?"

"Yeah," I say, wondering if this conversation is ever going to end.

"Cool. I'll see you tonight. I'll bring my dog."

Then he walks right past me.

"No, Brian. Wait, that's really not a good idea . . ." I begin to say, but I can tell he's not listening.

I don't think I can handle another night like the last one. Are there going to be people camped out at my house again tonight, disturbing my family, not to mention the whole neighborhood? How long is this going to go on? And more importantly, what can I do to stop it?

The rest of the school day is thankfully uneventful. I rush from the building at the end of the day to avoid being confronted by any other pet lovers or website viewers.

Still, I can't shake the creepy feeling in the pit of my stomach that things are only going to get worse in both these areas. And, in a way, they are connected.

It's bad enough having kids come up to me at school, telling me they now know secrets about me and messing with my reputation. But I'm also supposed to be a serious entrepreneur (at least, that's what Manny likes to call me), and I have reputation to think about there, too. I am the "Sure" in "Sure Things, Inc." and if people all over the world are going to trust our products, they're going to have to trust *me*.

At home I grab a snack, round up Philo, and head to the office. I arrive to find ten people standing in line, each one with a dog or cat. I don't recognize any of them.

"Are you the guy who can tell what dogs are saying?" one boy asks.

"Well, not me, precisely, but—"

"Who are you? Dr. Dolittle or someone?" another person asks.

"No, really, this is not the best time," I say, searching my mind to see if I can think of a "best time." I can't.

"Okay, we'll come to your house later tonight," says the first kid. "My friend was there yesterday and told me it was amazing! He never knew his cat liked belly rubs so much."

"No, please don't come to my house," I say as the crowd breaks up, but I can see that no one is in the mood to listen to me.

I slip inside.

Manny looks up from his work, starts to look down, and does a double take.

"Are you okay?" he asks, getting up from his desk, something he rarely does.

I must really look terrible.

"You look terrible!" he says.

Well, there you go.

"I've never seen you looking so stressed and exhausted," he continues.

"This is supposed to be a happy time for me—the launch of new product, Sure Things, Inc. moving forward . . . but I'm really stressed," I explain. "Between the people wanting to use the Cat-Dog Translator and the stuff that's on that website . . ." I can't even finish the thought.

"Okay, have a seat," Manny says, guiding me by the shoulder over to my workbench. "I'm going to get you a slice of pizza—you like jelly beans on your pizza, right?"

"Funny," I say, and actually it is since everyone in the world also knows this about me now. It's nice that one of us, at least, can keep a sense of humor about all this.

Manny returns and hands me a slice of pizza covered in colorful (nonpurple) jelly beans. I take a big bite.

"All right, I have a plan that I think will help solve two of your three big problems," Manny begins.

"*Three* big problems?" I ask through a mouthful of pizza. "I have three big problems? I thought I only had two."

"One's an older problem that we'll take care of by solving one of the newer problems," Manny clarifies. Now I really have no idea what he's talking about.

"You know how Principal Gilamon has been hounding you about Billy Sure Day?" Manny goes on.

"Of course," I say. "He brought it up the other day."

"So here's the plan. What if we set up an assembly where every kid who wants to know what his or her pet is thinking can find out all in one shot? They'll just bring their pets to the assembly and one by one, you can use the translator on them. That would stop a lot of people from coming around to your house at night, and at the same time satisfy

Principal Gilamon's desire for you to star in an assembly—to inspire hard work, creativity, and all that other good stuff he loves so much."

I remain quiet and munch on another bite of my pizza.

"And, of course, it would also serve as a major PROMOTIONAL EVENT for the upcoming launch of the Cat-Dog Translator. So, what do you think?"

"Do you think he'd go for it?" I ask.

"Principal Gilamon? In a heartbeat."

"Okay. See if you can set it up. And thanks, Manny."

"Anything for my partner!"

"Now, what about my third problem, the website?" I ask, not wanting to seem ungrateful, but I was still very worried about all these secrets floating out there.

"That's next up on my list, Billy," says Manny. "I promise. We'll figure that one out too."

I spend the afternoon cleaning up my workbench—or, at least what passes for clean to me. Then it's time to get Philo from the park—same bushes—and head home.

Riding my bike, I round the corner to my house and gasp at the sight of twice as many people lined up on my lawn as yesterday! And they've started showing up earlier!

I don't know what to do. I mean, I know what I'd like to do, which is to tell them to all go away. But I don't want any more bad publicity spreading about me, like how I'm mean and I wouldn't share my invention, and that sort of stuff.

Maybe if I take care of this now, everyone will go away and things will get quiet later on tonight. Standing on my front step, I power up the long range settings on the translator.

"Okay, everyone!" I shout to be heard over the barking, screeching, howling, and meowing. "I can't meet with you individually, but I'm going to turn on the Cat-Dog Translator for all of you. So please listen carefully for what your pet is saying. A reminder—the Cat-Dog Translator will only work on cats and dogs.

That's why it's called the Cat-Dog Translator. So, for those of you I see out there who brought rats, donkeys, snakes, and lizards, thank you for your interest, but I really can't help you."

I turn the power on. In a repeat of last night's noisy mess, the sounds of translated pet talk come pouring out of the speaker, all in a garbled stew of words.

I wait about five minutes, and when I can't take any more of it, I turn off the device, thank the crowd for coming, and head inside.

But throughout my homework and dinnertime I hear another round of pet owners gathering outside. By the time I go to bed, the nose is deafening. Manny's plan for the assembly better work, or I may never get to sleep again!

The next afternoon I walk into the office even more exhausted than before. Fortunately, Manny has some more good news—at least I think it's good news.

"I have a plan to trap the person behind the

website!" he says as soon as I walk through the door. "But it will require two things from you, Billy. Some acting, and A DISGUISE. What are your thoughts on fake mustaches?"

So many fake mustache choices!

Chapter Eleven

Sure Secrets Exposed!

"I DON'T KNOW IF THIS IS GOING TO WORK, MANNY," I say, glancing at myself in a mirror on the office wall. I'm wearing a big bushy fake mustache on my upper lip. It looks like somebody's gerbil jumped up onto my face.

I'm also wearing thick glasses, making it kind of hard to see, and a big floppy hat which droops to one side of my head. I must look ridiculous. Of course, I can hardly see what I look like through these dopey glasses, so I couldn't really tell you.

"You can pull it off," Manny reassures me.

Ridiculous!

"I'm not worried about you in the slightest."

Well, that makes one of us.

I slide the glasses down my nose a bit so I can peer over the top of them and actually get a peek at myself. I repeat: I look ridiculous!

"Manny, I look like a hairy, nearsighted old man!" I cry.

"That's okay," Manny replies calmly. "As long as you don't look like Billy Sure, this plan should work just fine."

"I hope you know what you're doing," I say. "Okay, so explain the plan to me again . . . one more time."

"You are going to go onto the Sure Secrets website and convince whoever is running it that you have the juiciest Billy Sure secrets he or she has ever heard," Manny explains. "Go ahead. It may even be fun!"

If I were to make a list of things I think might be fun, doing what I'm about to do would probably come in at #957 on the list—right below going to the dentist after eating roaches!

Manny hands me a piece of paper with a list of secrets he made up.

I sit next to Manny at his computer and bring up the Sure Secrets website. Just looking at it gives me the CREEPS.

"Okay, there's the contact button," Manny says, pointing to the upper right-hand corner of the screen.

I take a deep breath and click. A blank message box pops open. At the top of the box it says: "Tell us your Sure Secret!"

I look down at the piece of paper that Manny has given me and follow his script. I type: "I have the biggest secrets you'll ever hear about Billy Sure" into the message box.

"I hope you know what you're doing, Manny," I say again. Then I click send.

"Now what?" I say, scratching my nose, which itches terribly from the hairy beast sitting on my upper lip.

"Now we wait for an—"

DING!

The bell rings, indicating that a message has arrived. Just below my message, in another box, someone has written: "Do tell! Do tell!"

I look at Manny, impressed that his plan brought such an immediate reply, and thinking for the first time since he explained it to me that it might actually work.

"Perfect!" says Manny. "They took the bait. Now go ahead, send them the first 'secret.'"

I look at the paper and type what Manny has written there: "For starters . . . Billy Sure sometimes goes days without taking a shower!"

I turn to Manny. "That is gross!" I say.

"Just send it," Manny replies. "They're going to love it. It's just the kind of thing they're looking for."

"But it's not true!" I say. "Except for maybe sometimes."

"*They* don't know that," Manny explains, smiling and raising his eyebrows.

Sighing deeply, I hit send.

A few seconds later a reply appears: "I like! I like! Tell me more!"

"Oh, we got 'em now!" Manny says, obviously enjoying this way more than I am. "Go ahead, type the next one, but don't send it right away. Let them sweat for a minute."

I type: "Billy Sure walks around his house talking to himself. Sometimes he even has arguments with himself."

"You know that one's not true either, right?" I say.

"Of course I do, Billy," Manny says. "Okay . . . Wait . . . Wait . . . Send!"

I click send.

Instantly, the reply comes back. "Excellent. Go on!"

"Okay," says Manny. "This is it. The trap's been set. The bait's been placed. Now let's reel this big fish in! Go ahead and type the next one."

"For the final and most amazing secret of all to have its full impact, I need to be face-to-face with you. Time for a video chat?" I hit send.

Manny and I stare at the screen. Nothing. A minute goes by, then another.

"They're onto us!" I say, getting nervous that all this has been for nothing.

"Just wait," Manny says. "They're weighing their options, trying to figure out how to turn this to their advantage. They'll reply. We just have to be—"

DING!

"And here we go," says Manny.

"I'd prefer it if you wrote the secret out."

"That's weak," says Manny. "Very weak. Well, now is when we seal the deal."

"Okay," I say. "What does that mean? What do I write back?"

"I got this one," says Manny. "Just make sure your MUSTACHE is on tight."

"If it was on any tighter, it would be up my nose!" I say.

Manny takes over the keyboard: "If you're not interested enough in what I have to say to talk to me face-to-face, I'll just send this huge, earth-shattering secret to the local paper's business section, and they can be the first to embarrass Billy and Sure Things, Inc." He hits send.

This time the reply comes right away.

"Click on the video chat link on the Sure Secrets website, please," comes the reply.

"Okay, partner, you're on!" Manny says.

I position myself directly in front of the screen. I check my mustache, adjust my glasses, and straighten my hat. Here goes.

I click on video chat. A small window pops open within the website. A face fills the entire window. It is the face of none other than

ALISTAIR SWIPED, the CEO of Swiped Stuff, Inc., Sure Things, Inc.'s biggest rival! Alistair Swiped came out with the Every Ball, a rip-off of the All Ball, and he recently pretended to be my mom to rip off our other products.

I have to work hard to hold it together. I can't show my shock at seeing Swiped's face on the screen. I can't even let on for the moment that I even know who he is.

"Well," says Swiped, squinting at what must obviously be a pretty ridiculous-looking face (my face, that is) on his computer's monitor. He sounds slightly annoyed. "What is this great big secret that you will only tell me face-to-face?"

"Are you ready?" I ask, milking the moment for all it's worth.

"I'm ready!" shouts Swiped, now clearly annoyed. "Well?"

This is it . . . time for the big payoff.

I pull off the hat, take off the glasses, and yank the mustache off my face, practically taking my nose with it.

"I am Billy Sure!" I shout. "And you, Alistair Swiped, are *soooooo* busted!"

Swiped, whose face has been filling the entire chat window, stumbles back in shock, startled that he's been caught. With his face no longer taking up the whole window, I can now see Swiped's entire office. Sitting on his desk is the original Cat-Dog Translator prototype!

At that moment, Philo catches sight of Swiped's face. He starts barking wildly at the video chat window. I snatch the second translator prototype out of my bag, switch it on, and hold it up to Philo.

His barking comes out: "NICE MAN, GIVE ME ANOTHER TREAT. ANOTHER TREAT. I LOVE YOUR TREATS!"

Manny and I look at each other as the whole truth becomes clear. It was Alistair Swiped who stole the original prototype. He's been using it on Philo during Philo's long periods of time away from me each day. He's been bribing him with treats—which explains Philo's recent weight gain—and getting him to bark into the translator to reveal secrets about me. That explains why so many of the things that have appeared on the Sure Secrets website were things only Philo could have known.

Manny leans in close to his laptop's monitor.

"All right, Swiped, I'm only going to say this once," he begins. "If you don't return our prototype within the hour, the police are going to hear about your little theft. Not to mention our attorney."

The video chat window instantly closes. A few seconds later the entire Sure Secrets website vanishes, replaced by a message which reads, "This web address is no longer valid."

"All right, so we took care of the website," says Manny. "And by the way, great acting job. I definitely think that once you're old enough, you should grow a real mustache. It looks good on you."

I just smile and shake my head. "So how do we get the original prototype back?" I ask. "You told him to return it within the hour, but you didn't say where or how."

"I have a hunch," says Manny. "Let's just give him an hour, then follow me."

The next hour ticks by excruciatingly slowly. When it's up, Manny says, "Let's go."

He opens the back door, allowing Philo to dash out. We follow in time to see Philo easily hop over the backyard fence. Struggling to keep up, we follow Philo to the park. Not surprisingly, he leads us right to the same patch of bushes where I've been finding him every day for the last week.

Philo dives into the bushes, barking and moaning, obviously looking for the treats he's been getting from Swiped there day after day. Pushing the bushes aside, I spot the original translator prototype sitting on the ground. It has a note pinned to it that reads:

All right, Sure. Here's your stupid invention back. You win this time. But next time . . .

Chapter Twelve

You Can't Win Them All!

BACK AT THE OFFICE, AFTER SOLVING THE MYSTERY of the Sure Secrets website and Philo's disappearances, I feel very relieved.

"This has been weighing on me big time," I say to Manny.

"I know . . . one problem down, two more to go," says Manny. "And just in time, too. Here's an e-mail from Principal Gilamon saying that he thinks an assembly featuring your latest invention would be a great idea."

My relief suddenly turns to panic. I really don't like the idea of standing up in front of a packed assembly. But I know that Manny is right. This assembly will get Principal Gilamon off my back and get some of those pet owners to stop coming to my house at night.

Speaking of which, when I arrive home that evening, the usual crowd of owners and pets has gathered in front of my house. I recognize them as mostly kids from my school. Standing on my front step I announce: "Listen, everyone. I have good news. Next Tuesday morning at eight I will be leading an assembly at Fillmore Middle School. Students will have a chance to bring their cats or dogs up to the stage and find out what their pet is saying, using Sure Things, Inc.'s latest product, the Cat-Dog Translator. So good night, and I will see you next Tuesday."

I slip into the house. The crowd starts to break up. Manny would be so proud.

For the next few nights I sleep better than I have in a while now that the Sure Secrets website is gone. Then Monday night comes and I toss and turn, nervous about the assembly the next morning. I keep telling myself that once this assembly is done, kids will stop coming to my house with their pets, and we can start to move ahead with the mass production of the Cat-Dog Translator.

On Tuesday morning, bright and early, I find myself standing up onstage, holding the Cat-Dog Translator, standing next to Principal Gilamon. The auditorium is packed full of kids and their pets. Every student had to have his or her parents sign a permission slip to attend or bring a pet. Manny is watching from the back of the room, giving me thumbs-up signals. Principal Gilamon steps up to the microphone.

"Welcome, students, to this very special assembly," he begins. "As many of you know, we have a bit of a CELEBRITY attending Fillmore Middle School.

"Our own Billy Sure is an inspiration to us all. At the age of twelve he started his own company, which has grown into a great success. We can all learn from Billy's example of hard work, perseverance, and creative problem solving.

"Well, this morning we have a special treat

for you—even better than a dog treat. Billy has agreed to share his latest invention with us, the Cat-Dog Translator. So, what I'd like you to do is, if you have come with your pet, please line up along the right-hand aisle. Billy will use his invention to translate the barks and meows that your dogs and cats make into words we can all understand. Okay, Billy, take it away!"

Kids race from their seats, jockeying for position, forming a loud, unruly line down the aisle.

"Thanks, everyone, for coming and bringing your pet," I say. "Can we have the first pet up onstage, please?"

A boy steps up onto the stage with his dog.

"What's your name and what's your dog's name?" I ask.

"I'm Wilson, and my dog is Brownie," says the boy.

"Okay," I say. "Now I'm going to put the Cat-Dog Translator near Brownie. Let's see what he has to say."

I power up the device and move the

microphone close to Brownie's mouth.

"RRRRRIIIIIFFF!" he barks. Out comes: "WILSON THROWS MY BALL FAR!"

"Wow!" says Wilson. "That's amazing!"

The audience breaks into wild applause. I glance over at Principal Gilamon, who is clapping and smiling broadly. I catch Manny's eye at the back of the auditorium and can see him already counting our profits in his head.

Next up onto the stage is Judy Geralds, with her cat, Flick. Holding the translator up to Flick, we hear him say: "JUDY SCRATCHES UNDER MY CHIN."

Judy proceeds to scratch under Flick's chin. "MORE. . . . KEEP SCRATCHING. . . ."

Again, the entire auditorium cheers loudly.

A steady line of kids and their pets come up, one by one. The Cat-Dog Translator works perfectly. I'm completely convinced now that Sure Things Inc.'s next product is going to be a HUGE HIT.

Principal Gilamon walks over to the microphone. "I have a special surprise for everyone," he says. He turns to the side of stage and calls out: "Come here, Scout!"

A cute little dog comes trotting out onto the stage. A collective "AWWW!" fills the room.

"I brought my own dog, Scout!" Principal Gilamon announces. "I can't wait to hear what he has to say."

The auditorium bursts into applause again.

This should be kind of cool, I think. *I don't know anything about Principal Gilamon, except when it comes to school stuff.*

Principal Gilamon leans down and scratches the top of Scout's head. The little dog looks up lovingly, right into the principal's eyes. I put the translator near Scout's mouth. He barks, and out comes . . .

"YOU FART IN YOUR SLEEP."

The entire auditorium explodes into laughter. Principal Gilamon looks horrified. His face is as red as the beets my dad likes to put in his spaghetti sauce. He scoops up Scout into his arms and hurries offstage, returning without the dog a few seconds later, but still

You fart in your sleep!

looking very flustered, embarrassed, and—oh no—a bit annoyed with me, if I'm reading that look correctly.

Everyone is still laughing, and no one is laughing harder than the kid who comes up onstage next with his own dog.

"I'm Stevie and this is my dog, Paws," says the boy.

Holding the translator up to Paws we hear: "STEVIE LIKES TO HIDE HIS SISTER'S SHOES!"

"What!" shrieks a girl sitting in the audience. Everyone, including me, turns toward the voice and sees a girl standing and pointing up at the stage. "That's *you* who's been doing that?" she screams. "Wait until I tell Mom. You are in so much trouble!"

Stevie stops laughing and turns angrily to me. "Thanks a lot!" he snarls, then picks up Paws and hurries from the stage.

The room is still abuzz from the last two translations. Kids are laughing and chattering. Just my luck, next in line is none other than Allison Arnolds!

As she walks up onto the stage with her dog, Dusty, I get very nervous. I really hope she didn't see the Sure Secrets website.

"Hi, Allison," I say.

"Hi, Billy." So far, so good.

"Let's see what Dusty has to say."

Dusty barks. Out comes: "ALLISON SPENDS HOURS LOOKING AT HERSELF IN THE MIRROR EVERY SINGLE NIGHT."

"I do not!" she shouts, looking right at me, as if I was the one who said it. "Not every night."

Allison storms offstage with Dusty.

Great. Now she's mad at me too.

The mood in the auditorium is starting to turn ugly. Some kids are screaming at me, like I did something bad. Others are laughing and making fun of the kids who have had embarrassing stuff revealed about them. I know all too well what that feels like.

Amid the chaos, a girl named Stella comes up onstage with her cat, Loafer. I try to gain control of the unruly crowd, but it's hopeless.

I put the translator in front of Loafer.

"STELLA EATS EXTRA CAKE, AND THEN SHE PUTS THE CRUMBS IN HER BROTHER'S ROOM SO HE GETS IN TROUBLE," says the cat.

"Hey! No fair!" shouts Stella's brother from the audience.

Stella glares at me. "Why don't you turn that stupid thing off!" she yells before storming off the stage.

The chaos in the auditorium gets louder. Principal Gilamon has had enough. He walks to the microphone.

"Billy, I think it's time for you to leave the

stage with your . . . your . . . invention," he says, unable to hide the disdain in his voice. "This assembly is over! Everyone get to class!"

After school that afternoon I meet Manny at the office.

"Well, that was a DISASTER this morning," I say as Philo curls up on his doggy bed.

"Yeah, it could have gone better," Manny agrees.

We both sit in silence for a few seconds, neither of us wanting to say what we are both thinking. I finally break the silence.

"Manny, I don't think the world is ready for the Cat-Dog Translator," I say. It sounds correct coming out of my mouth, but it also makes me sad, thinking about all the work we have both put into this.

"I don't know, Billy," says Manny, but I can tell he has been thinking the same thing.

"Our pets simply know too much about us," I explain. "After what happened at the assembly today, not to mention the trouble with Swiped

and Philo, it's just too dangerous. Think of all the problems it can cause—the secrets that have no right to be revealed. Our pets simply know too much. Principal Gilamon has gone from my number-one fan to the president of the 'Say No to Sure Things' movement."

"That was pretty funny, you have to admit," Manny says, smirking.

"Not for Principal Gilamon, or the other

people who got embarrassed," I say. "Sure, we might sell a lot of these, but what do we do about the backlash? Sure Things' reputation is at stake with every product we put out."

"As much as I hate to admit it, I think you're right," Manny finally replies.

"Yeah, it's too bad, but at least we can keep the prototype so we'll know what Philo is saying."

"Well, it's actually more than just too bad," Manny says. "Without the Cat-Dog Translator, we're in a bit of trouble."

"What do you mean?" I ask, really not liking the sound of this at all. Manny is the most upbeat, optimistic guy I know. If *he* thinks we're in trouble . . .

"Sure Things, Inc. is now going to have to pay back all the money that Yummy in the Tummy pet food company has already invested in the promotion and production of the Cat-Dog Translator," Manny explains. "And, since we've already spent half of that money gearing up to manufacture the translator, we're going to have to dip into the profits from our other inventions."

Manny brings up a spreadsheet on his laptop, stares at it for a few seconds, then frowns.

"You know what this means, don't you, Billy?" he asks, looking up at me.

"I don't have to worry about Allison Arnolds finding out that I like her anymore?" I ask, hoping to lighten the mood a bit.

No such luck.

"No, Billy. It means that we need a new invention—and pronto—or Sure Things, Inc. could go OUT OF BUSINESS!"

This afternoon Manny and I are sitting in the world headquarters of Sure Things, Inc., otherwise known as the garage at Manny's house, trying to figure out our next move.

"What about getting some money from a bank?" Manny suggests as he scans four websites at once, checking out short-term loans, interest rates, and a whole bunch of other money-type stuff I really don't understand. "Or, like I said earlier, we could invent something new."

"What if we just went back to being regular kids again?" I ask. "You know, like we were before the All Ball?" I feel a small sense of relief having said this aloud, after testing it out in my head about a hundred times.

Manny stays silent, his focus glued to his computer screen.

"I mean, what about that?" I continue, knowing that if I wait for Manny to speak when he's this locked in to something, I could be waiting all day. "No more double life trying to be both seventh grade students and successful inventors and businessmen. How bad would that be to just be students again? It doesn't mean I can't invent stuff for fun, like I used to do."

I pause, giving Manny another chance to respond. No such luck.

"For me, it would just mean that I wouldn't have to live with the pressure of always coming up with the Next Big Thing, of always having to worry about how much money my inventions are going to make."

Still nothing from Manny.

"You know my routine," I go on. "Get up, go to school, go home to pick up Philo, come here, invent, go home, do homework, go to bed. Then get up the next day and do the whole thing again. I mean, what if I didn't have to do that anymore? Would that be terrible?"

I finish. I must admit these thoughts have bounced around my brain more than once during struggles with completing inventions, disasters like the CAT-DOG TRANSLATOR school assembly, and on stressful nights trying to invent while also trying to complete homework assignments on time.

Just as I wonder if Manny is ever going to speak again, he turns from his screen.

"I'm sorry, did you say something?" he says, straight-faced.

"I—I—" I stammer in disbelief. Did I really just go through all that for nothing? Did I share my deepest doubts and worries with my best friend, when I just as easily could have told them to Philo for all the help I'd get?

Manny cracks up and punches me gently in the arm. "I heard you," he says, smiling. "It's just that things were getting a little too serious around here."

"Well, what do you think?" I ask. I really do depend on Manny's advice. He's super smart and almost always knows what to do in a tense situation while remaining perfectly cool and composed. That is reason #744 why Manny is my best friend and business partner.

"You could stop being a professional inventor if you want," Manny begins in his usual calm voice. "But we both know that inventing is what you are best at. It seems to me that for you to be anything other than the world-class inventor you are would be cheating yourself, and the world, of your talent."

Hmm . . . I hadn't really thought about it that way.

But Manny is just getting warmed up. "You're lucky," he continues. "You know what you love to do. You know what makes you happy. You know what you're best at. And you're only twelve. Some people go through their whole lives and never figure out what they are best at."

As usual, what Manny says makes great sense to me. I guess I am pretty lucky that I already know what I'm best at. I start to think about people going through their whole lives and not knowing. It's kinda sad. I feel bad for them. Ideas start to whiz around and buzz through my brain.

"It would be great if we could help those people," I say.

And then—**DING! DING! DING!**—the lightbulb goes off for both of us. Manny and I look at each other and smile. The worry and indecision about my future dissolves in an instant.

"What if we invented something that would help people, whether they're kids or adults, know what they're best at!" I say, feeling energized by the idea. "I can see it now . . . a helmet or something that you put on your head that tells you what your best talent is. No more wondering what you're going to be when you grow up. With Sure Things, Inc.'s Best Test Helmet, you'll know what you should do for the rest of your life, the moment you put the invention on your head!"

Manny frowns. Uh-oh, he doesn't like it.

"Well, the slogan could use some tweaking," he says in a mock-serious tone that instantly tells me he's kidding. "We can just call it the BEST TEST. But . . . I LOVE IT!"

Leave it to Manny to snap me out of my funk and get me excited about a new invention. Now, of course, all I have to do is invent it!